# Life at
# Loon Lake

Ashley Lovette

# Dedication

*In loving memory of my mom, Marlene Lovette, who always encouraged me to chase my dreams and helped me develop the confidence to do so. I miss you each and every day.*

# Acknowledgements

I would like to express my deepest gratitude to my friend, and past colleague, Matt Larsen for helping me edit *Life at Loon Lake*. Without his expertise, this book would be seriously lacking in comma use, as well as an overall congruent structure. Thank you for opening that first file long ago and taking a chance to help a friend.

# Table of Contents

# Chapter 1

## School's Out

It was finally here.  The day Samantha Troman, known as Sam to her friends, had been anxiously waiting for.  Oakdale Middle School would be closing its doors for the summer beginning promptly at 3:30.  The past couple of weeks had seemed to drag on and on with the thought of summer as just a tease.  She could not believe that it would finally be here in 14 minutes.  In less than a quarter of an hour, Sam would be given 3 long, fun-filled months of freedom!

Sitting a couple of rows in front of her sat Logan Steel, her best friend and lake neighbor.  He was sitting straight, listening intently to Mrs. Morgan, Sam and Logan's fifth grade teacher.  She was giving her "I know you'll remember to study and read over the summer" lecture.  Come on!  Do teachers really believe that any normal 11 year old would actually think about school stuff when there was so much else to do?  Logan was probably the only student that was actually listening to Mrs. Morgan go on and on about "responsibility" and "not wasting time getting ready for sixth grade."  Sixth grade!  That didn't start until September and it was only the beginning of June!

Logan and Sam both lived near Loon Lake. Except for the lake itself, there wasn't much besides lots of farmland and dusty dirt roads. Logan's parents actually lived on the lake, but Sam's mom and dad lived across the road. Sam wasn't envious at all though because her grandma, Grandma Troman, lived right on the lake, across the road from her house. Sam could always be found at Grandma T.'s house, sitting in the treehouse out by the water. Now that she wouldn't have school, she could spend tons of time with Logan and Frankie, her other best friend, fishing and swimming and not thinking at all about story plots, compound sentences, or frustrating fractions.

"Rrrrinng!" rang the school bell announcing the end of the day. "Have a nice summer," said Mrs. Morgan in her no-nonsense voice as her students hurriedly rushed past her on the way out to the busses.

"Hey Logan! Wait up!" shouted Sam. Sam elbowed her way out into the hallway and caught up with Logan just as he was checking his locker for the *third* time to make sure he hadn't left anything in it.

"Do you see Frankie?" asked Logan. Both Sam and Logan scanned the fifth grade hallway in hopes of seeing their friend Frankie.

"Nah, don't see him," said Sam. "Let's go grab a seat on the bus and we'll save it for him."

Their bus driver, Miss Annie, smiled at them as they climbed up the steps. Miss Annie was pretty neat as long as you didn't do anything too upsetting. Today she looked more than ready to begin what would be her last route of the school year. Waiting in a seat about halfway back was Frankie with his Coca-Cola baseball cap on.

"About time," mumbled Frankie when he spotted Sam and Logan.

"How'd you get here before us?" asked Logan as he scooted in the seat, holding on to his backpack.

"I'm small so I can go through the crowds faster," answered Frankie pulling his hat down low to shade his eyes. Frankie was seated next to the window watching the other students from Oakdale Middle School hurry to their busses, or to the line of cars and trucks full of waiting parents.

Both Sam and Logan became inseparable friends with Frankie Ray last October. He had been riding his bike past the boat landing and noticed that Sam and Logan were fishing for bluegills on the bank. Frankie rode over on his beat-up, second-hand bike, turning circles and throwing up dust in the empty parking lot. He had never been fishing before and was curious. Both Sam and Logan were eager to show him all about it. They learned he was new in school and had just moved to tiny Loon Lake from great big Chicago. The three clicked together and have been inseparable ever since.

Sam plopped down onto the outer edge of the bus seat and held on tight to the seat in front of her as Miss Annie darted out onto Main St. She leaned back and tried to get as comfortable as possible to wait out the next 15 minutes until the Loon Lake kids would be dropped off.

"Hey Frankie, did Mr. DeWalter give some stupid speech to your class about reading during the summer and not forgetting school work?" asked Sam as she dug through her backpack to locate a piece of gum. Finding a pack, she offered a piece to Logan and Frankie, who both declined.

"Mr. DeWalter just had us clean our desks and help take down stuff in the classroom. He didn't even pretend to encourage us to study over the summer. It was a blow-off day." Frankie slouched down farther in his seat and continued to look out the window.

"Sam, you know it wouldn't hurt for you to read a book every now and then. You might actually like some of the stories in my paperbacks if you would just read past the first paragraph," said Logan.

Sam snuck a look at Frankie and rolled her eyes. Logan was what you would call a typical bookworm. He always had some paperback book that he was lugging around out in the boat or up in the treehouse. Sam chose to ignore Logan's concern about her lack of reading interest, and instead asked her friends if they wanted to meet at the treehouse after they got off the bus.

"I can," said Logan. "I'm sure mom will let me after I feed Oliver." Oliver was Logan's new kitten.

"You know me. I'm game." Shrugging his shoulders, Frankie glanced over at Sam and Logan and then returned his gaze to the window. Neither Sam nor Logan asked him if he thought his mom would care. They already knew that Frankie's mom wasn't like their moms. It didn't seem to matter to her where Frankie was or when he would get home. She never put up a fuss if Frankie got a bad grade on a project or didn't do well on the spelling test – which seldom seemed to happen even though he never studied. Frankie rarely talked about his mom or her boyfriend that lived with them. Sam and Logan never asked too many questions.

"What about you, Sam? Will your mom and dad let you head over to your grandma's?" asked Logan.

"Yeah, I'll be there," replied Sam. Logan looked skeptically over at Sam, but she didn't elaborate. Logan thought for sure she had said her mom told her she needed to clean her room before any more treehouse visits. He was pretty sure that Sam was up to one of her usual tricks, but he didn't ask her about it. He knew that if Sam said she'd be there, she would find a way.

The bus stopped at Oakdale Trailer Park and Frankie squeezed out of the seat and headed down the aisle with the Carley twins. He turned around halfway to the front and gave his friends a thumbs-up sign. They knew he'd be on his bike riding the two miles to the lake shortly after the bus left. A couple of more stops and it was Logan's turn to get off.

"See you at the treehouse," he said and headed off the bus and down the short driveway to his house. His mom was out working in her flower gardens. She stood up and waved a dirty gardening glove towards Sam who was now peering out the side window. Sam waved back and got ready for her stop since she was next. She watched out the window as Rascal, the Wheaton's big German Shepherd, raced by in hot pursuit of a rabbit. When the bus stopped at Sam's house, she practically skipped down the bus aisle in her excitement to finally begin summer vacation.

"Have fun this summer, Sam," Miss Annie said as she winked at Sam's freckle-faced reflection in the big driver's mirror that hung over the steering wheel.

"Don't worry, Miss Annie. I'm going to have a great summer break!" Sam said and headed down the steps and out the door. She was already planning the best way to get out of cleaning her room so she could head down to the treehouse.

# Chapter 2

## The Treehouse

"Samantha, is that you?" Sam's mom asked as Sam slammed the screen door behind her on her way in the house.

"Yeah, mom. I'm home," hollered Sam. She went to the kitchen and dropped off her backpack on the kitchen table.

"You can take that right up to your room, young lady, and start cleaning that mess you call a bedroom."

"I was thinking about doing just that mom, I truly

was, but then I remembered that other thing I promised you."

"What other thing?" her mom asked skeptically. She was in the middle of putting a pot roast in the oven and did not want to deal with Sam and one of her schemes.

"Well yesterday you asked me if I could take that casserole dish back to Grandma's and I promised you that I would as soon as I could. I've been feeling guilty all day that I forgot about it last night."

"Samantha Patricia Troman, I seriously doubt that you have been riddled with guilt on your last day of school over a casserole dish!" Her mom was standing in the kitchen with her hands on her hips giving her that "I know what you're up to" look. Sam was just beginning to wonder if she would indeed have to make a quick stab at cleaning her room when her father walked in from work. Saved! Sam could always fast talk her dad into going along with her.

"Hello ladies. Uh oh. Did I miss something?" asked her dad as he sat down and started to take off his boots. Sam quickly answered before her mom could say anything.

"I was just telling mom that I should take that dish over to grandma's house before she needs it. I was hoping that I could finish cleaning my room after I get back before I go to bed tonight." Sam tilted her head and gave her dad her best "endearing" look.

Sam's dad looked from his wife's face to his daughter's, and tried unsuccessfully to hide the grin that quickly came to his face. His carrot top, freckle-faced daughter was a constant delight and aggravation to him. He did not doubt for one moment that she was planning on heading to meet her friends and go fishing.

"Well Sam, you did promise your mom you would

work on that room. Though maybe she'll let you do the bulk of it when you get home from your grandma's if you pick up your dirty clothes and put them in the hamper before you leave."

Sam had a quick silent debate in her head before she decided that it looked like this was the only help she was going to get from Dad, which meant this was her best option. She looked pleadingly at her mom and said, "Mom, it is kinda like a holiday today, ya know, with it being the last day of school and the official beginning of summer vacation."

Sam's mom looked from her daughter's twinkling eyes to, ironically, the same pair of eyes on her husband's face and knew she was beat. "Go ahead." she said. "But don't forget to put those clothes in the hamper. And you will be cleaning that room from top to bottom when you get home this evening."

"All right!" Sam shouted as she raced up the stairs to quickly begin gathering her clothes.

"Samantha, try not to wake your sister. She's taking a little nap," Sam's mom said. She was silently thinking to herself that maybe having Sam head across the road to the lake for a couple of hours wouldn't be such a bad idea. It would give her the time she needed to finish the housework in peace.

Sam raced to her room and hurriedly grabbed all of the clothes that had somehow accumulated on her bedroom floor. Taking care not to wake Katie, her annoying 3-year old sister, Sam headed down the hall to the bathroom and haphazardly dumped the clothes into the already heaping hamper. Sam quickly grabbed a pack of gum that was hiding on her desk under a school notebook and headed for the door. Her mom was waiting at the bottom of the stairs with the casserole dish and a hug for her daughter.

"Be careful and be home before dark."

"Sure thing mom. I'll see you in a little bit," Sam replied quickly hugging her mom and racing towards the door.

"Hey Sam," shouted her father from the living room doorway. "Tell the boys I said hi and put whatever you catch in the live trap. I'll clean them tomorrow." He was grinning at her with his arms crossed and his eyes knowing.

"Bye Dad!" yelled Sam as she flew out the door and headed across the road to Grandma's.

Grandma Troman was sitting at the kitchen table with Logan with a plate of warm cookies when Sam showed up with the casserole dish. Sam didn't bother to knock, but just walked in and went over to give her grandma a big hug.

"Hi grandma, what ya doing?"

"Hi sweetheart. How was your last day of school?" Grandma asked returning the hug.

"Long. But I'm just glad it's over and now we have the whole summer ahead of us for fishing," Sam replied as she plopped down in one of the kitchen chairs and snatched a chocolate chip cookie. Her grandma always made the best chocolate chip cookies around. They were almost as good as grandma's homemade bread with strawberry freezer jam.

Grandma Troman meant everything to Sam. She was the type of grandma that was fun to be around. She loved kids, fishing, and the Detroit Tigers. She treated Sam and her friends as if what they had to say mattered - not like how some adults treated kids.

"Where's Frankie?" grandma asked.

"He should be here soon," replied Logan.

As if on cue, Frankie appeared outside the kitchen window with his bike.

"Frankie, we're in here," hollered Sam.   Frankie let his bike fall in the grass and headed over to the screen door.

"Come on in Frankie and grab a cookie." Grandma said.

"Thanks Mrs. T." said Frankie as he shuffled inside.

Grandma handed him a cookie and gave him a smile.  Frankie didn't sit down, but just continued to stand next to the door and eat his cookie.  Grandma smiled but didn't ask him if he wanted to sit down.  She seemed to understand that Frankie wasn't comfortable coming in to other people's houses and making himself at home.  In fact, Frankie had never been in Sam's or Logan's houses.  He only came into Grandma T.'s house.

Grandma sat with Logan and Sam for a couple more minutes and asked all of them some more questions about the last day of school, but she could tell that they were anxious to get to the treehouse.  On their way out, Grandma handed Logan a container of cookies and told them to grab a Coke if they wanted one.

"Thanks Mrs. Troman," Logan said, taking the container.

Sam opened up the fridge on Grandma's screened-in front porch and grabbed 3 Cokes.  Grandma was the only person Sam knew that had a fridge on her porch just for pop and worms.  Sam waved and ran out to catch up with Frankie and Logan as they headed out to the willow tree.  Grandma looked out and smiled after the group, loving the fact that she was a grandma, but also wishing she could capture that carefree attitude of children anticipating a summer full of adventure and excitement.

Logan reached the willow tree first and placed the

cookies in what the kids called "The Goodie Elevator" which was actually a bucket that Sam's father had rigged with a pulley system so that the kids could take things up to the treehouse easily. Sam caught up with him and placed the Cokes inside as well. Logan grabbed the rope that was wrapped around a nail in the trunk of the tree and pulled on the rope so that the bucket rose up into the tree next to the window of the tree house. Logan then wrapped the rope on the nail so that the bucket wouldn't move. Using the ladder, the kids then clambered on up into the tree house.

The treehouse itself was an ideal place for Sam and her friends to have as a headquarters of sorts. Sam's father worked as a construction worker and he was great at building things. He helped the kids build a sturdy, two-room structure that was rain proof and the envy of all the lake kids.

The ladder consisted of six pieces of wood nailed to the trunk of the tree that the kids could climb up. The ladder led to an opening in the floor of the treehouse that Sam and her friends could unlatch and push up to enter the house itself. Inside, the tree house main floor had two benches alongside a couple of the walls and a small table directly to the right of the opening in the floor. Sam and her friends could easily sit around the table and plan an adventure for the day or eat any goodies that Grandma Troman sent with them.

To the left of the floor opening was another room about half the size of the first one that the kids had dubbed "The Treasure Room." This was where the kids kept some of their more prized possessions. Logan had brought an old two-shelf bookcase that his parents were going to get rid of at a garage sale and placed it on one of the walls. He always kept a few books there in case he wanted to do some reading, which, to the dismay of Frankie and Sam, was almost always. Also, Grandma Troman had given them an old cricket box that she had found in her gardening shed and the kids kept that in the treasure room as well. From time to time they would go in search of insects to put in their box. There were a few other items: Frankie's favorite baseball hats, an old baseball and battered mitt, and a Walkman that was missing a double A battery.

Each room of the treehouse had one window. One of the windows directly faced out to the lake and the other window faced Grandma's house. The window facing Grandma's house was also the one that they opened to retrieve items from the Goodie Elevator.

Near the window that faced the lake, Frankie had nailed up a board to act as a small shelf. (He was good at that type of thing.) On the shelf, Sam had placed a pair of binoculars she had gotten as a birthday present when she had turned ten. The children were constantly checking up on a couple families of loons that made their home on the lake. They also liked to spy on any of the boats that may be out on the water. Alongside the binoculars sat a flashlight and a disposable camera Logan had received for his birthday. The flashlight came in handy for when they went worm or frog hunting after dark. The camera they had only used a couple of times to take some pictures of some baby geese when they first started to waddle around.

As if the treehouse wasn't cool enough, it had one more feature that made it absolutely fantastic in the children's minds. Sam's father had built a small opening under the floorboards of the treasure room. Two boards were not nailed down tight and allowed easy access to a secret compartment about the size of a 12 pack of pop. Anything that was top secret was kept in what the kids called "The Vault." All three of them knew the exact location of the vault and they had taken a secret oath to never tell another soul. An old braided rug that Sam had salvaged from her mom's scrap box was kept on the floor of the treasure room, strategically positioned over the loose floorboards so that any visitors to the treehouse would never know it existed. The only item in the vault right now was 12 tightly rolled up dollar bills. The kids had earned the money by doing some yard work a month or so ago for the Wheatons, the local farmers that had land surrounding part of Loon Lake.

As Logan headed over to the window to retrieve the cookies and pop, Sam sat at the table and Frankie went and plopped down in a beanbag chair in the corner.

"Well what should we do first?" asked Sam. "Should we take the boat and go fishing for some bluegills over in front of your mom and dad's Logan?"

"Well, if you wanted to be practical, we could just walk over. It would probably take less time." Logan sat down next to Sam and tossed a Coke to Frankie.

"Yeah, but not as much fun as taking the boat, right Frankie?"

"She's right," Frankie popped the top to his Coke and took a long drink. Frankie **loved** Coke. Sam always had a pack of gum with her, Logan was always carting around a book, but Frankie lived on Coke. It was the one thing his mom always had in the refrigerator. There could be days where you couldn't find a can of soup or a slice of bread, but the Coke was always there.

"Do we still have worms in the shed or are they in the fridge, Sam?" asked Logan.

"I saw a container when I grabbed the Cokes, but I know there are some in the shed with the fishing poles too."

The three sat around the table for a few more

minutes finishing their pops and talking about their plans to spend a lot of time in the tree house over the summer. After throwing their pop cans in a box in the corner, they headed down the ladder to get ready for fishing.

Sam, Frankie, and Logan walked over to the small storage shed that sat under the willow tree. Grandma Troman let them have one side of the shed and she had the other. Their side was just big enough to hold their fishing poles, the one tackle box they used, three life jackets, and a live net to hold whatever they caught. Grabbing the gear, the kids paused just long enough to grab and swing the rope hanging from a big bell positioned high up in the tree. The kids called this the "Boat Bell." One of the rules of the boat was that they always had to let an adult know when they were going out onto the lake, and they also needed to tell someone when they got back. Sam's dad had hung a bell from one of the outer tree branches so that Sam and her friends could ring the bell and then wait for Grandma to appear on the porch. If Grandma heard the bell, she would then wave to the kids and they would wave back. The same process was repeated when they returned from being out on the lake. This prevented them from screaming across the lawn and bothering snooty Mrs. Mayflower, the nosy busybody who lived next door to Grandma.

The kids climbed into the boat and rowed a few houses down to where the weeds dropped off in front of Logan's house. This was their second favorite fishing spot. The number one best spot to catch fish in Loon Lake, in their opinion, was over by where Old Man Starn, the Loon Lake outcast, lived. The kids called that area Cattail Cove because of all of the cattails that could be found over there. They knew, though, it was too late in the day to row all the way over there, and then have to head home before dark.

It didn't take long for them to catch about 20 bluegills and then head back to put the fish in the live trap that Sam's dad had tied to Grandma's dock. They parted ways with plans to come back tomorrow and fish on the other side of the lake. Sam left with thoughts of cleaning her room. Logan started walking home thinking about which book he would bring to the treehouse tomorrow to add to his collection there. Frankie hopped on his bike wondering if there was a can of soup at home to microwave for dinner.

# Chapter 3

# Old Man Starn and the Body

The next Tuesday afternoon, Logan, Sam, and Frankie were all sitting in the treehouse arguing about what to do. Each of them had different ideas. Logan wanted to start reading the fourth Harry Potter book, Frankie wanted to find something to eat in Grandma T.'s frig, and Sam wanted to go fishing.

"Sam, why don't we go tomorrow when we have more light?" asked Logan. He didn't want to get the life jackets and worms out if it meant they couldn't stay out for more than an hour or two. Logan was of, course, being practical as always.

"It's already a week into summer and we haven't gone to Cattail Cove yet," groaned Sam. It took about 15 minutes of steady rowing to get them over there, but it was usually worth it because of all the bluegills they could get in one spot. It was also nice and quiet and it kept them out of the view of Mrs. Mayflower's telescope. Mrs. Mayflower was the type of person that wanted to know *everyone's* business. She was constantly keeping an eye on the Loon Lake residents through the telescope in one of her upstairs windows. She had "thoughtfully" informed Grandma T. on more than one occasion of the kids' activities that she did not agree with.

"It doesn't matter to me," said Frankie. "Before we

go though, we should check and see if your grandma has any pretzels or chips we can take along."

"Well? How about it Logan?" asked Sam.

"Fine. But tomorrow we are going to have to go to the worm bed and fill our empty night crawler containers." Logan's family let him bury an old bathtub next to their shed so that the top of the bathtub was right at the top of the ground and this is where Logan kept his supply of worms. Logan had done some research online to find out what type of "food" to keep in the soil and how to take care of the worms so that they'd stay alive. The kids kept a worm container in the fridge on Grandma's porch, but they had to fill it up every now and then at Logan's house.

The kids scrambled down the ladder and headed in different directions to get what they needed to begin their trip. Frankie and Logan grabbed the fishing gear while Sam headed to the house to find out about snacks and grab some pops and the worms out of the fridge.

Once inside the rowboat, the kids did rock, paper, scissors to find out who would start rowing. Frankie lost and good-naturedly took his seat in the middle and began to row.

The lake was quiet. Weekdays were typically slow anyway with very little boat traffic, but today Loon Lake seemed especially empty. The boat skimmed over the water easily and left tiny ripples on the water. Frankie rowed past the public landing where only one rickety blue truck was sitting with an empty boat trailer. He headed past a couple more houses and then reached the woods.

Loon Lake was unique to other lakes in the area in that only half of the lake had houses on it. The other part of the land surrounding the lake was owned by the Wheatons. They were farmers and the property had been in their family for 3 generations. Sam's mom was always saying that if she was Bob Wheaton, she'd make a lot of money by selling some of the woods or pasture ground that bordered Loon Lake. Sam's dad disagreed with her. He always said that the wooded and pasture side of the lake made the lake nice for fishing and just enjoying the water. Bob Wheaton must have agreed with Sam's dad because he never showed any intention of selling parts of his property. The only time that anything had been sold was many, many years ago before Sam was born. Sheldon Wheaton, Bob Wheaton's dad, had sold a small wooded lot to Mr. Thomas Starn, or as the kids referred to him, Old Man Starn. It was somewhat of a mystery to many of the kids of Loon Lake why Mr. Wheaton would sell a lot in the middle of his land to Mr. Starn (who was well known as mean and disagreeable.) The way the kids figured it, very few adults ever did anything that made sense anyway.

Frankie's turn with the rowing was up and Sam took over. The kids had it figured out exactly where they had to switch so that each did their fair share of rowing. Sam made sure that she took her turn rowing right along with the two boys. She wouldn't have thought to do otherwise.

When they got to Cattail Cove, Logan let down the anchor slowly so he didn't scare all the fish away, and Frankie put the live net with the collapsible top into the water. Sam filled a small bucket with water that they could use to help clean their hands when they needed it. Each did their part with a practiced ease that comes with the experience of fishing together often. Bobbers in the water, the children sat in a companionable silence and waited for the fish to bite. Each was lost in their own thoughts.

Sam always enjoyed herself when out on the water. She looked around and spotted the family of loons weaving in and out of the clusters of swaying cattails. She quickly pointed them out to the boys and asked if anyone had thought to bring the binoculars. They said they hadn't and continued to fish. Sam glanced at her friends and rolled her eyes. She wondered if they actually spent any time looking around them at the beauty of the lake. In fact, she would have been quite surprised to find out that each them did enjoy the lake as much as she.

Frankie would never have believed that a place so peaceful actually existed. He never tired of Loon Lake. He loved fishing, but it didn't really matter to him as it did to Sam and Logan whether or not he caught anything. He loved the serenity that Loon Lake offered. No slamming doors or harsh words spoken out on the lake. That didn't mean that it was always quiet. The large part of the lake always seemed to have a speed boat or two stirring up waves, but that didn't matter. The lake always gave him hope that despite everything, some things turned out alright.

Logan was wishing he had brought his book. It looked like he was paying attention to his red and white bobber, but he was actually watching a grey egret make its way on tall, skinny legs down a bank in search of food. Egrets were a favorite of Logan's. He knew that Sam preferred the loons and Frankie always seemed interested in the muskrats that would swim around carrying sticks to their homes, but for Logan it was the egrets that were special. He wished fervently that he was an artist. He would sketch the bird as it just started to take flight, with its wings outstretched skimming the water's edge. The particular egret he was watching was dipping its head every now and then in search of small fish to eat for supper. It looked like a pretty good life to Logan, although he truthfully couldn't find any fault with his own.

About 25 bluegills and a few small perch later, the friends agreed that the trip had been successful and it was time to pull up anchor and head in.

"Hey guys. What's Old Man Starn doing?" whispered Frankie. He was trying to be extra quiet so that his voice wouldn't carry as well over the water. He didn't want Old Man Starn to hear him.

Logan and Sam turned to look over at the gray, weathered house nestled in the middle of the birch trees that belonged to Old Man Starn. He was walking backwards across his small yard, pulling a green tarp to the edge of the woods. It looked like from the way he was straining that whatever was in the tarp was heavy. Sam whispered, "See, we should have brought the binoculars."

"Shh!" both Logan and Frankie turned to Sam. At the same time, Old Man Starn looked right up across the lake to the boat and stopped walking. It seemed like forever as everything stopped and the kids sat frozen to their seats. Old Man Starn was staring directly at them, giving them a look that sent shivers down to their toes.

Frankie was the first to recover. "Logan, start rowing," commanded Frankie.

Logan did not need to be told twice. He grabbed the oars and put everything into getting them across the lake. Sam and Frankie kept looking over at Old Man Starn who had begun again to drag the tarp a bit deeper into the woods. He stopped and picked up something from the ground.

"Sam, what's he doing?" asked Logan who was still rowing with all of his might even though they had passed the point where it was time to switch.

"I'm not sure. I can't really make it out."

"I know what he's doing. He's digging a hole," said Frankie. "The only question is what's in the tarp?"

Logan momentarily paused in rowing and quickly glanced over to the woods and saw OMS tossing shovels of dirt into what appeared to be a growing dirt pile. He quickly resumed rowing, heading straight for the treehouse.

Sam looked from one best friend to the other. "There's only one thing that would be so heavy. Old Man Starn is burying a body."

# Chapter 4

# Derrick and the Dare

"I'm sure it wasn't a body," Logan said adamantly.

The next day, the three friends were gathered around the table in the treehouse talking about the events of the previous evening. By the time they had got back to Grandma Troman's and tied up the boat after their fishing trip the day before, there had been little time left to talk. After Sam had rang the Boat Bell, Grandma hollered out the window that both Logan and Sam's parents had called to ask for Grandma to send them home after they got back from being out on the lake. They had all left silently, each one thinking about Old Man Starn and the green tarp. They had agreed to meet the next day to discuss what they had seen.

"What else could it have been?" asked Sam as she opened a can of Coke. Frankie grabbed one from the middle of the table and did the same.

"I don't know, Sam, but it doesn't make sense that it's a body," Logan stated. Logan was feeling as if he and his friends would be better off forgetting the whole incident. Logan did not like to stir up trouble and that seemed to be just what Sam was trying to do. Besides that, Logan really did not believe that OMS would be burying someone out in his woods. It sounded like something that he would read about in one of his fiction books.

"We know the stories about Old Man Starn. Are you forgetting about Tyler Sampson's experience last Halloween?" (Tyler was a kid in Sam and Logan's class that told everyone at school that OMS had chased him with a knife.)

"Oh, come on Sam! Tyler's weird and you know it. There's absolutely no truth to that story," replied Logan.

"Maybe. Still, it's almost like this was bound to happen. I wonder who it is?" said Sam. She plopped down on one of the benches and propped her head in her hands on the table.

"Has anyone been missing lately?" asked Frankie. He wandered over to the window that looks out onto the lake and began to look through the binoculars at a group of geese gathered on the shore near the landing.

"Not that I know of," said Sam.

Logan seriously thought his two best friends had lost it. Not only were they talking about a lake neighbor burying a body, they were actually trying to rationalize who could have been in the tarp!

"Sam, even your grandma says that Old Man Starn should be left alone," said Logan. "I heard her say once that he chooses to live over in the woods because he likes his privacy."

"Well, Grandma doesn't know about the tarp with the body, does she? Besides, old people stick up for each other. That's a well known fact."

Frankie momentarily stopped his study of the geese and looked up at Sam. "That's not true. Your grandma doesn't stick up for nosy Mrs. Mayflower." Frankie liked Grandma T. and he wasn't going to let anyone say anything bad about her, even if it was her granddaughter.

"She's different. Grandma knows the truth about Mrs. Mayflower because she lives right next door with her gang of cats. Grandma can't help but see that she's a mean old witch."

"Sitting here all day arguing about what we saw isn't going to solve anything. What we need to do is walk down to the store and see if we can get any information from Mr. Meets," said Frankie, putting down the binoculars and joining Sam and Logan at the table. Mr. Meets was the owner of The Loon Lagoon, a small store on Loon Lake's north shore. He was also the only grown-up aside from Grandma Troman that actually treated the three as if what they had to say was important.

"Hey, that's a great idea. I don't know why we didn't think about it sooner," replied Sam. "Let's go."

After Sam told Grandma T. their plans, Logan grabbed a dollar from the vault and the three headed down the dirt road for the ½ mile walk to the store. The Loon Lagoon had only two vehicles in the parking lot when Sam, Logan, and Frankie walked up to the door. One of the vehicles was Mr. Meets' old brown truck. The other was a new, candy apple red sports car.

"Hey guys, look. Derrick's parents' car is here," said Frankie. "I wonder how Derrick the Deranged is doing?"

Derrick Baker was known as a spoiled rich kid. He attended Oakdale Middle School and was in the same grade as Sam and her friends. Derrick was also a Loon Lake kid. His parents owned a big, beautiful 2-story brick house with lots of windows that was on the lake not too far from Logan's house. Derrick always got everything he wanted and he didn't mind bragging about it to others. The trio did not get along well with Derrick, especially Sam, and they tried to avoid him as much as possible.

"If we're lucky maybe he stayed home," replied Logan. None of the three wanted to ruin their trip to the store by having to deal with Derrick.

"Hi Mr. Meets," said Sam as she walked through the door. The bell above the door jingled cheerfully as the kids entered the store.

"Well, if it isn't Samantha. And there's Logan and Frankie right behind you. How are you guys doing? Have you been catching all the fish out of my lake?" asked Mr. Meets. He had a soft spot for the mischievous Samantha Troman and her two friends.

"Don't you know Mr. Meets that the fish aren't safe as long as the three of us are around," replied Sam grinning at him over the counter.

"Well now, that's what I hear. Are the three of you having a nice summer?"

"You bet," said Frankie as he headed towards the open live-bait cooler that held buckets of tiny minnows. Frankie liked to go over and watch the minnows all swimming in the same direction. Every now and then he would dip his hand in the buckets and watch the minnows swim around his fingers. They definitely did not have stores like this back in Chicago.

"How's that grandma of yours, Samantha?" asked Mr. Meets. "She hasn't been in here lately and I was going to talk with her about the game last night." Mr. Meets and Grandma had a constant friendly dispute over which baseball team was superior, the Detroit Tigers or the New York Yankees. Grandma was a huge fan of the Tigers while Mr. Meets believed that the Yankees were unstoppable.

"She's doing great. We just came from there," replied Sam.

Logan walked over next to Frankie and looked into the buckets of swirling fish. Sam decided that now was as good a time as any to find out about Old Man Starn.

"Mr. Meets, you know Old Ma... I mean Mr. Starn don't you?" asked Sam

"Of course I know Thomas Starn. He's lived on this lake for over 30 years. Why do you ask?" Mr. Meets looked up from stocking the cigarettes behind the counter and gave Sam a questioning look.

"Well, I was just wondering, it's kinda weird isn't it? I mean the way he never talks to no one and lives all alone in the woods?" asked Sam.

"Sam, I don't know what you're up to, but leave Mr. Starn alone," replied Mr. Meets giving Sam a hard stare.

"Oh, I'm not up to anything, just curious is all," replied Sam as she tried to look nonchalant. Logan and Frankie headed back over to the counter and joined Sam.

"Mr. Starn just likes his privacy Sam. That's all. He doesn't need to explain to you or anyone the reasons for why he lives the way he does."

"Well, I know but he never seems to have anyone over at his house. You never see any family members and he's never in Oakdale shopping at the grocery store," answered Sam. She was starting to get frustrated. She thought for sure that Mr. Meets would be on her side.

"I don't think that Mr. Starn has that many family members left. That's why they don't come to see him. And he does come into town every now and then. Don't you think it'd be kind of lonely to have had most of your family members pass away? Maybe what Mr. Starn needs is a few friends to look out after him."

"I suppose so," said Sam. She looked over at

Logan and Frankie and gave them a skeptical look. She was hoping that Mr. Meets did not think that she was going to sign up to befriend the local outcast. That certainly wasn't going to happen any time soon.

Logan grabbed three suckers and put them up on the counter. He took out the carefully folded dollar he had stuck in his blue jeans and gave it to Mr. Meets. Mr. Meets rang them up and handed the change back to Logan.

Mr. Meets winked at Logan and looked at him and Frankie. "Are the two of you keeping her out of trouble?"

"That's a full time job," answered Frankie. He elbowed Sam good naturedly and she grinned at him. Sam turned to grab a sucker that Logan was handing her and she spotted Derrick leaning against the candy counter sneering at her. He must have been listening the whole time. Sam gave him a glare and then turned back and headed out the door with her friends.

"See you later Mr. Meets," said Logan.

"Yeah, good bye," said Frankie.

"Tigers rule, Yankees drool," hollered Sam.

"Yeah, that'll be the day," Mr. Meets said with a smile as he began to ring up Derrick's dad's order.

Outside of The Loon Lagoon, Sam and her friends took off their sucker wrappers and threw them out in the trash can near the store entrance.

"Hey Carrot Top. What are you and your *girlfriends* doing today? Playing house up in your grandma's tree?" sneered Derrick as he headed over to lean against his parents' car. His dad was still in the Loon Lagoon talking with Mr. Meets.

"Look Logan, it's Derrick the Deranged," Frankie said to Logan with a sarcastic smile on his face. "Now my day is complete."

"I'm sure it is," replied Derrick. "It's not every day

you get to be around someone like me." Derrick crossed his arms over his chest and gave them a look that told them

he thought he was too good to hold a conversation with them.

"Isn't that the truth," mumbled Logan.

"What was that?" asked Derrick taking a step forward.

"Oh, nothing. I was just agreeing with you Derrick," said Logan. Derrick was giving Logan a questioning look. He wasn't sure if he heard right, but he was going to let it pass.

"I heard you guys in there talking about Old Man Starn."

"Just making conversation, nothing important," said Sam. "Come on guys, let's head back."

"Sounds good to me, nothing to keep us here," replied Frankie. All three headed towards the road to begin the walk back to the treehouse.

"And here I was going to ask you about a challenge, oh well. It would be too much for you three to handle anyway." Derrick turned around and walked over to the passenger side of the sports car.

Sam spun around and headed back. "He's not worth it, Sam. Just let it go." Logan said as he grabbed Sam's arm. Sam shook her arm free. She had that glint in her eye that told Frankie and Logan that she wasn't going to back down from a challenge. Frankie smiled at Logan and shrugged his shoulders. He headed after Sam with Logan halfheartedly following. Sometimes Logan felt like he was always the only sane one of the three.

"What kind of challenge?" asked Sam.

Derrick smiled. He anticipated that it would be Sam who would be interested. "In two weeks the annual

Kid Fish Tournament is happening. There can be two kids to a boat. How about entering and having a friendly wager? My cousin Drake is coming to stay for part of the summer and we are going to enter together. Two of you guys could sign up and we could see who would win between us."

"What kind of wager?" asked Sam. She seldom was able to pass up a dare.

"The loser has to put a pail of fish guts on Old Man Starn's front steps without getting caught." Derrick smiled at Sam and raised his eyebrows. "How about it?"

"You're on," responded Sam without any hesitation. Frankie was smiling at Sam for taking the dare, but Logan had a whole different expression on his face. He looked as if he was going to get sick at any minute. Just as Logan was getting ready to speak, Mr. Baker walked out of the store.

"Hello, kids. Are you guys enjoying the nice weather?" Mr. Baker asked.

The kids mumbled a reply and turned to head back to the treehouse. Mr. Baker's car drove past and they could see Derrick grinning at them in the passenger window of the car.

"Sam, what did you do that for?" Logan was fuming now that he found his voice again. "We do not need to be messing around with Old Man Starn, especially given the current situation."

"I couldn't back down from that creep," replied Sam, kicking at a rock alongside the road. "Besides, I thought you were the one saying that OMS wasn't burying a body. Anyway, Logan you know we can't lose a fishing tournament. This is our lake."

Logan looked over at Frankie to try and reason with him, but he knew it would be a waste of time. Frankie and Sam were both itching to take on Derrick and his cousin in this tournament. He was beginning to think he would have been better off staying at the treehouse dreaming about Hogwarts.

# Chapter 5

# The Stakeout

As with everything, Logan believed in preparation as the key to success. The kids now had two things to think about; one being OMS and the supposedly "dead body," and the second was beating Derrick and his cousin in the fishing tournament that was taking place in two very short weeks. The three decided that the possibility of a murder was more of a priority. While Frankie and Sam were talking about getting the boat ready and heading over to Cattail Cove to do a stakeout, Logan was sitting in the treasure room busily writing.

"At least there won't be anybody to bother us today. The lake is empty and so is the landing," Frankie said while staring out the window at the lake.

"Yeah, well let's get going. I want to get over there and see what's happening," said Sam impatiently.

"Why are we doing this again?" asked Logan.

"We need to know what's happening. We can't just let Old Man Starn bury people in his woods. We are going to head over there and figure out what's going on. Maybe we'll find some evidence that will tell us what he's been up to." Sam folded her arms across her chest and glared at Logan. "Frankie and I are ready to go. What are you doing writing at a time like this?"

"If you insist on going through with this, we'll need a plan," answered Logan.

Sam looked up with interest showing on her face. "What kind of plan?"

"Well, I've been making a list of things we'll need to take over there if we are going to case the joint," replied Logan.

Sam raised her eyebrows at Logan's words while Frankie tried unsuccessfully to hide a laugh with a cough. He caught Sam's eye and mouthed, "detective books." Sam started to laugh and Logan quickly turned around.

"What's so funny?"

"Nothing. Nothing at all. Read away," Sam replied.

"Well, I'm sure you've already thought of this, but are you taking the binoculars?" asked Logan.

"I hadn't thought about that, but I guess it would be a good idea," mumbled Sam.

"Also, you will want to have paper and a pencil to write down anything unusual. We should take your Polaroid camera in case we need to take any incriminating photos. We will want our sunglasses because the sun is going to be in our eyes, and of course, we are going to have to take our fishing poles, worms, you know…the usual."

"Wait a minute. We are going over to spy on OMS and you want to go fishing?" asked Sam.

"We need it in case we get caught or someone suspects us of spying," chimed in Frankie.

"Frankie's right. We also have to have a cover story for your grandma and we might be sitting over there for a few hours with nothing to do. We may as well catch some more fish so your dad can have another fish fry."

"Okay, okay. Let's grab everything and get going. If you keep adding to the list, we won't be able to fit everything into the boat."

After the three had everything stowed away, Logan rang the Boat Bell, waved at Grandma T., and pushed away from the dock. Sam took her turn first at the oars and rowed steadily towards the far side of the lake. Frankie sat on the front seat, untangling a knot in the fishing line on his pole, Sam was in the middle rowing, and Logan was in the back, organizing some notes.

"Where should we anchor?" asked Frankie. He had undone his knot and was now switching seats with Sam so that he could take his turn at rowing.

"I think we should anchor right up near his boat. That way we'll have a good view on everything that's happening around the house," answered Sam.

"The only problem with that is he won't do anything wrong if he knows we're there were we can see him," Frankie pointed out.

"Let's go over by the first group of cattails near the corn field. We will be able to see most of what's happening with the binoculars and he won't suspect anything, since we usually fish over there anyway," Logan stated. He had already been thinking over the best location for the boat and had decided that this was it.

Sam and Frankie agreed with Logan. Frankie rowed the boat over to the spot and Sam dropped the anchor.

"Now what?" asked Sam. She was looking over towards Old Man Starn's house as if she was expecting to see him come out his front door waving a knife.

"Now we fish," answered Frankie. He pulled his hat down to shade his eyes as he casted out his line in the direction of a group of lily pads.

Sam looked over at Logan. He had already started to meticulously weave a squirming worm on the end of his hook. Resigned to the fact that there wasn't much she could do right now, Sam grabbed her pole and started to get it ready.

The three sat silently in the boat, alternately watching their fishing poles and Old Man Starn's house.

"What do you think he's doing in there?" asked Sam.

"I don't know. Could be anything," answered Frankie.

"He's watching the news," said Logan. Logan sat his fishing pole down and started to write on the pad of paper he had brought.

"How do you know he's watching TV?" asked Sam.

"Listen," replied Logan.

Sam stopped fidgeting with her pole and listened. Sure enough, Sam could faintly hear Weather Dan giving his 5-day forecast.

"Not bad. You're pretty good at this," said Sam.

Logan grunted and set his writing pad down. He picked up his pole and reeled in the bluegill that had swallowed the hook while he was busy taking notes.

"Do you think he watches the news every day?" wondered Frankie.

"I don't know. Maybe he's just been watching it lately to see if anyone has been reported missing. That way he'll know he needs to cover his tracks," answered Sam.

"Maybe he's just like every other old person and gets a kick out of watching the news," replied Logan. "A lot of people watch the news every day and they aren't murderers."

"I know. I know," answered Sam.

The three sat for another half hour without noticing anything happening at OMS's place. After about 30 minutes though, Old Man Starn came out of the back of his house and walked to a shed that was near the bank.

"What's he doing?" asked Sam.

"I don't know yet," replied Frankie. He had the binoculars and was trying to see into the small opening in the door of the shed.

OMS emerged seconds later with a bucket in his hand. He started to walk towards the dock, paused, and looked out onto the lake.

"Look natural, look natural," said Logan frantically gripping his fishing pole so hard that his knuckles were turning white.

Frankie dropped the binoculars so that they fell to his neck, held there by the string attached to them, and he quickly picked up his fishing pole. Sam hastily turned to face the opposite direction of OMS's house. In doing so, she knocked over the tackle box so that it hit the floor of the boat with a big crash.

"Oh great. We're all dead," mumbled Logan. He was staring at his bobber without even noticing that it was bouncing around like crazy with bites.

"He's walking again," whispered Frankie.

Sam and Logan both chanced a glance towards Old Man Starn's house and watched as he dipped his pail into the water and then continued to walk towards his house. He stopped at a plant near his backdoor and poured the water onto the ground.

"He's just watering something," said Logan. "Let me see the binoculars, Frankie."

Frankie handed Logan the binoculars and reeled in a small perch that had been biting at his worm.

Logan peered through the binoculars for a closer look at the plant OMS had watered.

"It's a tomato plant," said Logan.

"Who cares?" answered Sam. "We aren't learning anything by sitting here watching him water his vegetables."

"Actually," said Logan looking at Sam, "a tomato is a type of fruit."

Sam gave Logan a look that told him she didn't care at all if a tomato was a type of vegetable, fruit, or a new form of chocolate. All she cared about was that they weren't getting the evidence they needed to prove that OMS was up to no good.

After another hour of fishing and no activity at OMS's house, the three decided to call it quits and head back to the treehouse.

"We didn't find out anything," complained Sam as she sat down at the treehouse table.

"We know he watches the news," said Frankie.

"We also know that he was in his house for the 2 hours we were out there and he didn't get one phone call. We would have heard it," said Logan.

"How does that help us prove that he buried a body?" asked Sam impatiently.

"It doesn't. We'll just have to keep trying. We can't give up now," said Frankie.

"I guess we'll have to plan more stakeouts if you guys are serious about trying to find evidence about what was in the tarp," replied Logan looking from Frankie to Sam.

"Well then that's just what we're going to have to do," said Sam.

Logan just shook his head and neatly stacked his notes on the bookshelf in the treasure room.

"Maybe you should keep those notes in the vault so that no one sees them on accident and wonders what we're up to," said Sam.

"Good thinking," replied Logan. He removed the rug and lifted the floor boards that allowed him access to the secret compartment. He carefully folded his notes and returned the boards and the rug.

The friends said goodbye and headed home. They had already planned when they were going to make their next attempt at spying on Old Man Starn.

Sam, Logan, and Frankie tried two more times that week to go and spy on OMS  Both times they went, they were unsuccessful in learning anything new. They would have been bored out of their minds if they hadn't caught an occasional fish. The only thing they confirmed is that he watched the news at noon and that his mail was delivered around 10:30 A.M. The friends knew that if they wanted to find out anything new, they were going to have to come up with a different method of gathering information.

# Chapter 6

# Plan B

After three unproductive stakeouts, the kids were not any closer to finding out information about OMS than they had since when they first saw him with the tarp. They were gathered around the table in the treehouse on a Saturday morning, trying to figure out what to do next.

"Maybe we should go to the police. They can go and dig up Old Man Starn's yard and see what he buried," said Logan.

"That won't work," answered Sam. "First of all, they aren't going to believe a bunch of kids, and second, we don't have any evidence. All that we saw was OMS dragging a green tarp."

"I suppose you're right," replied Logan.

"What we need to do is get closer to him. We need to somehow get into his house," stated Frankie.

"Are you crazy!?" Logan cried giving Frankie an incredulous look. "Do you want to end up in a tarp six feet under!?"

"Whatever happened to, 'I'm sure it wasn't a body?'" asked Frankie. "Are you changing your mind?" Frankie finished the Coke he had been drinking and threw the can into a trash can near the bench.

"I don't know what I think anymore, but trying to get into the house is crazy. Are you talking about breaking in?"

"No. We can't do that. I am talking about being invited inside the house," replied Frankie.

"Are you telling me that you got an invitation in the mail for lunch at Old Man Starn's house. I'm feeling let down because he must have forget to add me to his guest list," Logan gave an exasperated look to Frankie and went to grab the pretzels that were still in the goodie elevator.

Sam rolled her eyes at Logan and turned to Frankie. "What do you mean? Do you have an idea?"

"What if I'm looking for my cat 'Fluffy,' and I take a flyer with a description on it around to some of the lake people?"

"You don't have a cat," said Logan. He returned to the table with the pretzels and put them in the middle.

"That doesn't matter. No one knows that but us. I could pretend I have a cat that has been missing. Sam could use her family computer and create a flyer that gives a description of 'Fluffy' and a phone number."

"Whose phone number would we use?" asked Logan.

"That's easy. We'll use my old one. It was disconnected a few weeks ago."

"Why was your phone disconnected?" asked Sam.

Frankie shrugged, "Mom forgot to pay the bill. Anyway, now we just use her cell phone."

"What would we do for a photo?" Logan asked. "We don't have an extra picture of a cat lying around."

"We'll just give a description, no photo. If anyone asks, we'll tell them we only had a picture of when she was a kitten and that wouldn't have helped," replied Sam getting excited about the idea.

"It might work," replied Logan. "But, how are all of us going to get into the house?"

"I think I should be the only one to go," said Frankie looking at Sam and Logan. He was anticipating an argument on this part of his plan and he wasn't disappointed.

"Why you?" asked Sam. She stood up from the table, put her hands on her hips, and glared at Frankie. "I might want to go too." Logan sat quietly at the opposite end of the bench. He figured that if Sam and Frankie were volunteering to go, he wouldn't have to, and that was okay by him.

"Sam, listen. It's supposedly my cat. If all of us went it would look too fishy. He already has probably seen us spending a lot of time over near his house on the lake. Also, we need someone back here in case something happens. I figured we could use those two-way radios your dad gave us," replied Frankie.

Logan still wasn't too sure of this new plan. He could see some definite flaws that needed to be worked out. "Speaking of something happening, have you thought about that? You would be going into his house alone, with him. And, you still haven't explained how you are going to be asked in," stated Logan.

"After I show the flyer and begin explaining why I'm there, I'll start coughing like crazy. He'll have to offer me some water or something. Grown-ups are always asking kids if they need some water when they begin coughing. While I am in the kitchen, I can quickly look around, check for some clues. If I think he's going to try something, I'll call you quickly on the two-way radio. I really don't think he's going to try to hurt a kid that's missing his cat."

"It's a great idea!" replied Sam. "When are we going to do it?"

"Hold on a second," said Logan giving Sam an exasperated look. "The flyer needs to be created, we have to think about when the best time would be, the radios need to be charged, we need to practice our codes…"

"Codes? What are you talking about?" asked Sam.

"Well, you know. What if Frankie's in trouble, what does he say over the radio?" replied Logan.

"How about 'Help! He's trying to kill me!'" answered Sam.

"Sam, this isn't funny. All I'm saying is that we can't just send Frankie over there without being prepared."

"He's got a point," replied Frankie. He didn't mind being the one to go over to OMS's, but he was counting on Logan to help figure out the details.

"Besides that, I have to go home in a little bit. My parents are going to my grandparents' house and I have to go with them," said Logan.

"Yeah, I gotta go too," said Sam disappointedly. "Mom told me that I couldn't spend all day over here. I think we're going shopping for some yard stuff that Dad needs. I don't think I can come over tomorrow either. Mom said something about visiting Aunt Bobbie." She looked miserable at the idea of having to postpone the adventure until another day.

"I guess I can stay home and watch TV or do whatever for the next couple of days," said Frankie. He hated feeling like he had nothing to do or no one to spend time with when Logan and Sam did things with their families. Sometimes he joined them when they had cookouts or shopping trips, but he couldn't go all the time. He would just be in the way.

"You could check things out on your bike if you had the time. You know, see if anyone goes in or comes out of Old Man Starn's driveway," said Sam.

"Yeah. That would give me something to do for the next couple of days," Frankie liked the idea of continuing to monitor OMS's activities. He felt useful that way. He thought he may even drive around the lake and see if it looked like anyone had been gone a long time from their home. He could look for lawns that needed to be mowed, newspapers piled into newspaper boxes alongside the road, or just something that looked out of place.

The three made plans to meet back at the treehouse Monday around noon. Sam figured this would give her enough time to work on the flyer. They could then finish hashing out their plan and decide on the best time to put it into action.

Sunday came and went with little activity happening around OMS's driveway. Frankie alternated his time between watching Old Man Starn's place and riding around the neighborhood looking for clues of someone missing. He didn't see anything out of the ordinary. The only lawns that needed to be mowed were the same ones that always needed to be mowed. He spent part of Sunday evening at the boat landing, watching families load and unload boats. When people weren't using the landing, he would wade into the water and watch the minnows swarm at his feet. He knew he couldn't do anything else to help figure anything out about OMS, but he didn't want to go home yet.

Grandma Troman spotted Frankie at the boat landing (her house was sandwiched between the landing and Mrs. Mayflower's.) Grandma waved Frankie over and asked him if he'd like to have a sandwich and some chips.

She was eating out on the picnic table looking out onto the lake.

"Thanks, Grandma T.," said Frankie as he grabbed a ham sandwich off the paper plate on the picnic table.

"Where's Logan today?" Grandma Troman asked as she got up and went to grab a couple of Cokes for Frankie and herself out of the pop fridge.

"He had some stuff to do at his house," mumbled Frankie between bites.

"Oh. I see. Well I'm glad I saw you over there at the landing. I was getting kinda lonely and needed someone to share my supper with." Grandma opened the bag of chips and took a handful to put on her plate. Frankie grinned and did the same.

The two sat and talked about fishing for a little bit while finishing their sandwiches. Grandma T. told Frankie that she was just getting ready to watch the Tigers and he could join her if he wanted to. Frankie declined, saying that he had to get home.

"Frankie, would you mind taking these chips with you?" asked Grandma T. "I really didn't care for them and I'd hate for them to just sit on my counter top going stale." Grandma Troman handed the bag out to Frankie as he was hopping on his bike.

"Thanks, Grandma T.," Frankie said. "I'll see you tomorrow. Thanks for dinner." Frankie waved and headed out the driveway onto the road headed home.

Grandma T. waved back and sadly shook her head. She gathered up the empty paper plates and pop cans and headed into the house. She was hoping that the Tigers had a good night so that she could go and tease Gary Meets about it the next day.

# Chapter 7

## Looking for 'Fluffy'

The following morning, the friends were gathered in the treehouse ready to begin Plan B in finding evidence against Old Man Starn.

"Well, here it is," said Sam. She plopped down in the bean bag chair in the Treasure Room of the treehouse and handed a copy of the flyer to Logan. Sam reached into her jeans pocket and pulled out a pack of gum. Logan grabbed the flyer and sat down at the table. He was appalled at what he read:

## Lost Cat!!

### A small cat was lost arond Loon Lake last Friday.

<u>Discription:</u> Yellow and black stripped like a tiger.
She has half an ear on one side and a short tail.
Walks with a limp.
Her name is Fluffy. Very Friendly.
She likes to chase birds.

If you see her, please call Frankie at #569-3061.

## P.S. There will be a $5 rewardd for the safe return of Fluffy.


"What," said Logan, "is this? Don't you have spell check on your computer?"

"What's wrong with it? Did I misspell something?" asked Sam shoving a piece of gum in her mouth.

Frankie went over to stand behind Logan and read the flyer for himself. "Looks good to me," said Frankie giving Sam a thumbs-up sign. He really didn't see what it mattered if Sam's typing skills weren't the best.

"Sam," Logan sighed ignoring Frankie. "This flyer is riddled with mistakes. Besides that, you gave an exact description of the stray cat that is always hanging around everyone's garbage cans. People aren't supposed to recognize 'Fluffy.' She's not supposed to be able to be found. She doesn't exist!"

"I didn't describe that cat on purpose. I guess I was just thinking about her when I was typing up the flyer." Sam shrugged and glanced at Logan. "Does it really matter? Frankie's only going to show the flyer to a few neighbors – just enough to make it look real."

"I guess you can just go back into your saved copy and make the changes," replied Logan grabbing a pencil off the shelf in the Treasure Room getting ready to make corrections on the flyer.

"Don't write on that!" said Sam sitting upright and grabbing the pencil from Logan. "I didn't save it on the computer."

"You didn't save it?" asked Logan in disbelief.

"No, I didn't. I also don't have any more paper to put in the printer. We ran out. So, all we have is this flyer here and the one I have in my pocket." Sam reached into her jeans pocket and pulled out a haphazardly folded piece of paper. Frankie took it and started smoothing it out, doing his best not to glance at Logan's horrified face.

"Good as new," said Frankie holding up the second, slightly wrinkled copy of the flyer. He thought it was best to change the topic.

"When should we go through with this? When's the best time of day?" said Frankie looking at Logan for the answer.

"I think you should go over there a little after noon time," replied Logan looking at Frankie. "That way, he'll already be sitting in front of the TV, and he may be so interested in what he's watching that he won't hesitate to ask you in when you start your coughing fit."

"That makes sense. At least we know he's going to be there and it's broad daylight," said Frankie. "Who's the neighbor that we're going to give the other flyer to?"

"I've been thinking about that," replied Sam. "It has to be someone that will let other people know what we're doing. We need others to know so that it doesn't look like we're targeting OMS. The other person has to be someone who likes to gossip with other neighbors." Sam looked at her friends. "There's only one logical choice. I'm sorry for it, but that's just the way it is." Sam sat down on the bench next to Frankie and gave him a friendly pat on the shoulder.

"Oh, man," said Frankie. "I really didn't want to have to go and talk with *her*."

"You're going to have to do it," stated Logan with an empathetic look on his face. "Sam's right. Mrs. Mayflower is the most logical person for the other flyer."

"You know," said Sam snapping her gum, "we could do this today. It's only 11:00 A.M. We've got plenty of time to get Frankie ready to go over to OMS's."

"I think she's right," commented Frankie before Logan could shoot down the idea. "We've wasted enough time on trying to figure out what's going on. I may see something or I may not. Either way, we'll have at least tried."

"What about charging the 2-way radios? We can't do this without them," said Logan.

"I did that the other day," answered Sam. "I was thinking ahead. I thought you'd be proud of me." Sam smiled and looked over at Logan.

"I am pretty impressed that you were thinking ahead," replied Logan. "Okay. If you guys think we can do this, then let's get started."

The three spent the next half hour arguing and planning on what Frankie would say and do when he got to Mrs. Mayflower's and Old Man Starn's. They decided to go ahead and conduct a test run with Mrs. Mayflower since they had some time before Frankie could head over to OMS's.

"What are we going to tell your grandma and our parents?" asked Logan.

"Don't worry about that. I'll tell Grandma later that we are trying to rescue the stray cat so that Frankie can give it a good home. She'll eat that right up. I'll also tell my parents the same."

"I don't know," said Logan. We don't want to lie to them."

"Look. It's not really like lying. The flyer doesn't actually say that Frankie owns 'Fluffy.' It just kinda implies it. Our parents won't see the flyer because we only have the two. It'll be fine." Sam gave a reassuring look to Logan and went to go and grab the walkie talkies. "Logan, if it bothers you, why don't you just tell your parents you're helping Frankie find a cat. There's enough truth in that for it to work."

"Yeah, okay. I guess that'll work." Logan picked up the wrinkled flyer and handed it to Frankie. "Are you all set?"

"Yeah, I think so," replied Frankie.

"Here's a walkie talkie," said Sam.

"Sam, I don't really need that right now. I'm only going next door. The only danger I am in over there is getting a lecture."

"Just take it. We need to practice," answered Sam.

Frankie reluctantly grabbed the walkie talkie and then stuffed that and the folded flyer into his pocket.

"We'll be watching," said Logan who had grabbed the binoculars off the shelf.

"Okay. Here I go." Frankie headed down the ladder and walked around the privacy fence Grandma T. had installed. (She had found that the fence was a definite necessity to living next to Mrs. Mayflower.) Frankie walked up the marigold lined sidewalk and rang Mrs. Mayflower's doorbell. He was secretly hoping that maybe no one was at home, but he wasn't so lucky.

"Yes, young man? What can I do for you? I don't want to buy anything, you know," Mrs. Mayflower came to the door in one of her many flower covered dresses. She peered at Frankie over her bifocals and waited impatiently for him to tell her why he was there.

"Um…I wanted to ask you about a cat," replied Frankie. He had momentarily forgotten the reason why he was standing there.

"You want to know about one of my babies?" Mrs. Mayflower asked glancing behind her at what appeared to be at least 6 or 7 cats that were lounging in varying positions over a couch and two extremely pink recliner chairs.

"No. Nothing like that." Frankie pulled out the crumbled flyer and handed it to Mrs. Mayflower. "I'm looking for my cat Fluffy. She's been missing for a few days and I was wondering if you've seen her."

"You're missing a cat. Oh, dear." Mrs. Mayflower quickly scanned the flyer, glanced at Frankie and gave him a disapproving look.

"Did you say what grade you're in young man? What is your name?" Mrs. Mayflower demanded.

"Um… Frankie, Frankie Ray. I'm going to be in the sixth grade in the fall."

"I know you. Your one of those kids that spends all that time up in the willow tree next door. Hmmm. Well Frank, did you know that there are some spelling errors on this flyer that any child even in fourth grade should be able to spot." She gave him another stern look. Frankie was spared whatever she was going to say next when the phone rang.

"Oh, that'll be my daughter. Come in, come in. I'll only be a second."

"Mrs. Mayflower I don't really need to …"

"Hurry up, Frank. I need to talk to you about this so-called flyer."

Frankie didn't see any way he could get out of it. With a glance towards the treehouse, Frankie shrugged his shoulders and walked inside.

"He's going in!" shouted Logan from his look-out in the treehouse.

"What?" Sam poked her head completely out of the window and looked towards Mrs. Mayflower's front steps.

"Where'd he go?" asked Sam looking at Logan.

"I told you. He went into the house. We're just going to have to wait." Logan pulled the bench closer to the window and made room for Sam. "You watch the windows and I'll keep an eye on the front door."

Meanwhile, in the house, Frankie was looking around in disbelief at the inside of the living room and kitchen. Every spot available in the room had something in it. There were more end tables, chairs, knickknacks, and stuff than he had ever seen before in his life. Despite the amount of things in the house, the interior itself was pretty clean. Everything seemed to have a spot, and despite all the clutter, there wasn't one speck of dust anywhere.

Mrs. Mayflower was standing in the kitchen talking into the phone and glancing every now and then in Frankie's direction. After a quick goodbye to the person on the other end of the phone, Mrs. Mayflower headed back to the living room where Frankie stood waiting.

"Now then. You say you're missing your cat. This description sounds like a stray I have seen stalking around the neighborhood." Mrs. Mayflower gave a questioning look to Frankie and waited for him to answer.

"She does sometimes wander around where she's not supposed to be. Fluffy usually comes back though every night. I haven't seen her for a few days now."

"Yes, well. I'll keep an eye out for her. I may even ask some other people I know to do the same."

Frankie stood quietly without changing the expression on his face. Inside he was smiling. He was sure that Mrs. Mayflower would do just that.

"Thanks, Mrs. Mayflower. I should really get back now." Frankie headed towards the front door with the intent on escaping the stifling house.

"Frank, wait a second. I wanted to ask you about your family. I know a lot of people around town. Do I know your mother or your father perhaps?" asked Mrs. Mayflower fishing for information.

"No, I don't think so."

"Well, maybe if you just told me where you lived, I …" Mrs. Mayflower trailed off at the sound of yet another phone call. "Oh, dear. I should probably get that. Maybe you could just wait a few more minutes…"

"Sorry Mrs. Mayflower. I gotta get going." Frankie took his chance to escape while Mrs. Mayflower reluctantly headed back towards the kitchen. She looked torn between learning more about the mysterious family of 'Frank' and answering her phone.

"Thanks for helping Mrs. Mayflower," shouted Frankie from the steps as he closed the front door behind him.

"Treehouse calling Shorty. Do you copy?" Frankie grinned and grabbed the walkie talkie out of his pocket. "Sam, I'll be there in a second." Frankie stuffed the radio back into his pocket and walked out and around Grandma T.'s house and into her yard. In less than a minute, Frankie was scrambling up the ladder and emerging from the floor of the treehouse only to face questions flying at him from both Sam and Logan.

"What happened?" asked Sam.

"Did everything go okay? What did she say?" inquired Logan.

"Just a second. Just a second." Frankie sat down at the table with his friends and readjusted his Coca-Cola hat.

"Have you guys ever actually been in her house before? Very weird, I'm tellin' you."

"I've been in there once with Grandma," said Sam. "We were dropping off some mail that had been put in

Grandma's mailbox by mistake. It's kind of crowded in there, huh?"

"You're telling me. I don't think she could cram anything else in there if she tried," said Frankie.

"Why did you go in?" asked Logan.

"The phone rang and she asked me to follow her into the house," said Frankie. "I couldn't just stand there looking like an idiot on the front steps, so I followed her."

"What did she say about the flyer," asked Sam. She was pretty proud of the flyer herself and wanted to see what Mrs. Mayflower had thought.

"Well, she caught on quickly that it was a description of the neighborhood stray."

"Of course she did," said Logan giving Sam an 'I told you so' look.

"It was easy to explain that though," said Frankie. He quickly told his friends about the conversation he had with Mrs. Mayflower about 'Fluffy,' and how she had asked about his parents.

"She asked you about your family?" asked Logan.

"Yeah. She was just being nosy. It frustrates her that she doesn't know who my parents are." Frankie shrugged his shoulders and grinned at his friends. "I wanted to tell her that my dad is a tight-rope walker for the circus and my mom works as a fortune teller on the carnival circuit. That would keep her guessing for awhile."

"It would serve her right," replied Sam folding her arms across her chest. "She thinks she knows everything that goes on around here. One of these days we're going to have to figure out a way to get her really good."

"I'm in," said Frankie.

"Well, I hate to break it to the both of you, but pulling a prank on Mrs. Mayflower is going to have to wait." Logan was looking at his watch and visibly wincing.

"It's 5 minutes to 12:00 and we've got OMS to deal with. The visit to Mrs. Mayflower's is going to be a walk in the park compared to going over to Old Man Starn's." Logan grabbed the other flyer from the table and handed it to Frankie.

"We won't be able to see you this time," said Sam. "Are you sure you don't want me to go with you?"

"No, Sam. I don't think it would look right. He would know something was up," said Frankie. He took his radio out of his pocket to make sure it was turned to Channel 5 along with the radio that would be left in the tree house. "I think I'm ready."

"Okay. It'll take you a little less than 10 minutes to get to his driveway. Once there, you need to 2-way us to let us know of your position," said Logan. He was glancing over his meticulous notes, checking to make sure they weren't forgetting anything.

"I'll let you know when I get there."

"Remember to switch to Channel 3 if you hear anyone else using the radios. Also, don't use real names," cautioned Sam.

"Sure thing Red," said Frankie using the code name for Sam. Frankie had adopted the name Shorty, and Logan, who had been very excited about choosing a name for the radios, was going by Rambo. (Frankie and Sam both thought this was hysterical, but they kept it to themselves.)

Frankie headed down the treehouse ladder and took off on his bike towards OMS's. Sam went to the table to sit and wait while Logan grabbed a fresh piece of paper and pencil to take down any notes from any information that Frankie can tell them. The two-way radio was sitting in the middle of the table.

"I'm here," crackled a voice over the radio a little while later.

Sam grabbed the radio before Logan could get to it. "Sounds good Shorty. Be careful."

Logan yanked the radio away from Sam and pushed the button on the side. "Shorty, this is Rambo." (Sam rolled her eyes.) "It's exactly 12:07. It's a good time to make your move."

"Okay. I'm off. I'll talk to you in a little bit." Frankie shoved the radio in his pocket and started to pedal down the narrow, dirt driveway, skirting around mud puddles and rocks. He couldn't yet see the house because of the windy path of the driveway and all of the birch trees on the property.

After a couple of twists and turns, Frankie got his first glimpse of the front side of OMS's house.

Frankie's first thought was one of complete isolation. The over-grown birch trees encircled the house in the same way a campfire ring surrounds a fire. The only break in the trees was where Loon Lake bordered OMS's property.

The house itself was in relatively good condition for its age. The wood exterior was gray and weathered. It was small, but it looked cared for. Someone had taken the time to paint the shutters black and plant colorful annuals in the pale blue window boxes. The overall effect was a cozy little house that didn't necessarily welcome intruders, but was proud enough to look the best it could.

Frankie slowly pedaled his way towards the front door and propped his bike against a pine tree near the sidewalk. Taking a deep breath, Frankie approached the steps and reached for the doorbell. Before he could reach his hand out to push the button, the front door swung wide open. Old Man Starn stood on the other side of the screen door staring down at him.

Thomas Starn stood glaring out of the screen door with a scowl on his face. His scraggly beard was as silver grey as the abundance of hair on his head. He was so tall that he towered in the doorway. Despite the warm weather, OMS was wearing a flannel shirt that looked as if it needed to be thrown away and a holey pair of jeans.

"What do ya want?" he bellowed.

"I…um…I wanted to…" Frankie pulled the flyer out of his pocket and handed it to Old Man Starn. "Here."

The screen door creaked open and OMS grabbed the piece of paper from Frankie. As Old Man Starn was reading, Frankie glanced over towards the garage and noticed a bundle of rope and chopping ax leaning against a rusty gas can. He visibly gulped and turned back to face OMS who was giving him a suspicious look.

"So, you lost your cat," stated Old Man Starn.

"Um, yeah. I was hoping that maybe you could tell me if you've seen her." Frankie gave a thin smile and tried to casually peer around OMS and look into the kitchen area. As Frankie leaned over to the side to get a better look, OMS stepped over to block his view.

"I can't say as I've seen this cat around here. Sorry." He started to hand back the paper, but Frankie shook his head.

"No, no. You keep it in case you see her later and need to call me. I'd really …" Frankie stopped in mid-sentence and began to cough uncontrollably. "I'd really appreciate it." Frankie continued his coughing and began to double over, clutching a hand dramatically to his chest. Old Man Starn was standing blocking the doorway, giving Frankie a questioning look.

"Water," gasped Frankie. "Is there a chance I can get a drink of water?" Frankie looked up to the towering man and gave his best pleading look.

"You sure can."

"Thanks," said Frankie hoarsely. He started to step up to the door, but OMS didn't move away from his spot. Instead, he gave a wry smile and pointed towards some bushes to the right of the door.

"You can use the hose right over there."

"Oh. Thanks," said Frankie. He gave a last feeble cough and, not knowing what else to do, walked and turned on the spickot hidden behind the waist high shrubs. As he was bending down to unravel the hose from the rocks near the side of the house, Frankie noticed something shiny reflecting the afternoon sun. Frankie hesitantly reached out to touch the half hidden object when OMS came walking up behind him.

"There it is." Old Man Starn reached down and grabbed what happened to be a long fillet knife out from under the bushes. "I must have lost it when I was rinsing off my fish filleting board the other night." OMS rose up to his full height, gripping the sharp knife in one hand and extending the other hand out to Frankie. "Do you need help up?"

"No thanks. That's okay." Frankie ignored the offered help and scrambled up to turn off the hose. He didn't even realize that he had not taken a drink.

"Well, I see your cough is gone."

"Yeah, I'm as good as new." Frankie gave a weak laugh and scrambled out towards his bike.

"I guess I better go," said Frankie. He stumbled over a rock lying in the driveway in his haste to get to his bike.

"I'll call you if I see anything," said Old Man Starn.

"What?" Frankie gave him a dazed look at first not understanding what OMS was talking about. "Oh, yeah. Okay. Thanks." Frankie hopped on his bike and raced down the driveway leaving a perplexed Old Man Starn still standing outside in the yard.

Frankie did not stop pedaling until he spun onto the road and past three more mailboxes. Only then did he pull off into the ditch and dig into his pocket for his walkie-talkie.

"It's me. I'm here."

"Shorty, is that you? Red to Shorty, do you copy?" Sam said into the radio.

"Yeah, this is Shorty. I'll be at the base in about 10 minutes."

"Shorty this is Rambo. Are you okay?"

"I'm fine. I'll be there in a few minutes."

"Okay. We'll talk later," said Logan.

Frankie stuffed the radio back into his pocket and continued his short ride back to Grandma T.'s house. He skidded into the driveway in record time.

"He's here and he's in one piece," said Sam from her lookout at the window.

Frankie hastily clambered up the ladder and flopped into the bean bag chair. He was breathing heavily from his hurried bike ride.

"Well?" asked Sam. "Tell us everything."

Frankie spent the next half hour giving his friends a description of what happened and his impressions of OMS.

"Holy Cow!" exclaimed Sam. "He was holding a knife over your head?"

Frankie and Sam continued to talk excitedly about the incident while Logan sat at the table in a subdued silence.

"Now we should be able to go to the police," stated Sam.

"I don't think we can," mentioned Logan from his spot at the table. Both Sam and Frankie turned to give him an incredulous look.

"What do you mean you don't think we can?" demanded Sam. "We have proof now. Frankie saw the knife. He practically *touched* it."

"Sam," said Logan shaking his head sadly. "It's all circumstantial."

"Circumstantial my butt!" shouted Sam. "What about the rope and the ax? How about the bloody knife?"

"Bloody?" Logan looked up with interest. "It was bloody?" he asked Frankie.

"Well, no. I didn't actually see any blood."

"Because OMS washed it off!" said Sam.

"Yeah, from cleaning fish Sam. At least that's what Old Man Starn told Frankie and it does make sense. Frankie was over by the hose where a person would clean off knives and pans from cleaning fish." Logan shrugged his shoulders and looked at his friends. "We have to look at this with an open mind. All of the items Frankie saw could be found in my parents' garage or yours. Heck, they could probably be found in your grandma's shed."

Sam dropped down on the floor next to Frankie looking discouraged. "I know your right," she said after a few moments. "What can we do though? The fact is OMS *was* burying something. All of us saw it."

"Why don't we just concentrate on keeping an eye on him?" said Frankie. "We have the Kid Fish Tournament coming up and we really need to start thinking about that, especially considering the consequences of losing to Derrick the Deranged."

All three friends started thinking about what it would be like to have to take a pail of fish guts over to

OMS's house. Logan outwardly groaned and looked as if he was going to get sick.

"I think Frankie is right," said Logan. "We can't risk anymore trips to OMS's house. Not after how things went with this visit to find 'Fluffy.' We're going to have to let off a little bit and do some more observations from the boat."

"We're not going to get anywhere," predicted Sam.

"Maybe, maybe not. At least we'll still be alive," said Logan.

# Chapter 8

## Grandma Knows Best

The next couple of days came and went without anything exciting happening. The three friends spent some time after the Plan B fiasco just fishing off of Grandma Troman's dock and going swimming at Logan's house. The friends also went over to Cattail Cove for a quick "fishing trip" but they didn't see anything unusual at OMS's house.

On Thursday afternoon, the kids were exploring the bank at Grandma's house searching for frogs and turtles. They weren't sure what they were going to do with them, but it was something to pass the time. Grandma was up towards the house working with her flowers.

"Kids!" yelled Grandma T. "Could you guys come up here for a second?"

"Coming," shouted Sam. Logan set the bait bucket on the dock and the three walked up to the house.

"What's up Grandma?" asked Sam as the three approached the flower pots Grandma T. was working with.

"I was wondering if you three wouldn't mind helping me for a minute." Grandma T. smiled at the three dirty faces and pointed towards a couple of large, ceramic flower pots bursting with bright red geraniums. "I need to put those two pots on my garden wagon. I want to put them near the front steps and spruce it up a bit. I was thinking that I could lift them myself, but no such luck."

"We can help," said Sam. She went over to help Grandma with one of the pots while Frankie and Logan lifted the other one and placed it into the wagon. The group then pulled the wagon across the yard, around to the front of the house.

"Beautiful flower pots always remind me of the neighbor lady who lived near my parents' house when I was growing up," said Grandma as they stopped the wagon near the door. "Her name was Mrs. Morney and she *loved* flowers. She had every kind imaginable surrounding her house and lining her driveway." Grandma helped Sam set one of the flower pots on one side of the steps and motioned Frankie and Logan to position the other pot on the opposite side.

"Anyway, Mrs. Morney, or who my brother Rex and I called Mrs. Ornery, was constantly yelling at us about not getting anywhere near her precious flowers. She especially loved iris plants. She collected a variety of colors that she ordered from specialty catalogues." Grandma T. smiled to herself at the memory. "Boy, she loved her irises."

"You called her Mrs. Ornery?" asked Sam as she sat down on one of the steps. She was awed by the idea of her grandma as a young girl.

"You bet," said Grandma T. studying the pots from a few feet away. "Hmm. Not quite right yet." She went over to continue to fidget with the pots while Frankie and Logan plopped down on the grass to listen to Grandma Troman's story.

"Mrs. Morney would stand on her front porch and shake her bony finger at us as we played catch or tag in the yard. One time, I remember, my brother and I were playing and Rex was running to catch a ball I had thrown. He was looking at the ball and wasn't paying any attention to where he was going. Of course he just had to trip and fall right into her beloved iris patch. I'll tell you, we knew we were in for it."

Grandma gave one final turn to the flower pot and stood back with her hands clasped in front of her. "There. I think that's good, don't you?" asked Grandma smiling.

"Looks good, Grandma," replied Sam.

"Grandma T., what happened after your brother fell into the flower patch?" inquired Logan.

"Well, there was no use denying to anyone what had happened. Our goose was cooked, so to speak. We told our mom what happened since we knew she'd find out anyway. She made us walk over and apologize to Mrs. Morney." Grandma Troman sat down next to Sam on the steps and took off her gardening gloves. "We were terrified," Grandma T. said with a little laugh.

"Did she yell and scream at you and your brother?" asked Sam.

"Actually, no. She was strangely calm when we explained what happened. Somehow that scared us even more. Both Mrs. Morney and our mother decided that the best punishment was for us to spend two entire Saturdays with Mrs. Morney helping her with odd jobs around her house."

"Two whole Saturdays!" exclaimed Sam horrified at the idea. "That wasn't fair. It was an accident!"

"You're right. It was an accident, but we had known better than to play catch over near her flowers. We didn't like the punishment, but we didn't have any choice. The next two Saturdays were spent with Mrs. Morney. Ironically, they didn't turn out as bad as we had thought."

"What did you have to do for her?" asked Frankie. He had been quietly sitting there in the grass listening closely to Grandma T.

"Mrs. Morney made us work in some of her flower gardens. She taught us what was and wasn't a weed. We learned all about the differences between annuals and perennials. While we worked with her, she would tell us about the flowers and explain some of their different uses for medicine or perfumes, you know, things like that. I can tell you that Rex and I hated it at first, but after the first few hours we became interested in what we were doing." Grandma smiled and looked as if she was lost in her own thoughts. "She gave us each a marigold in a small, plastic pot to keep at our house." Grandma T. stood up and dusted off her clothes.

"Grandma, why did you even keep that old marigold? I would have thrown it right into the trashcan," said Sam.

"Oh, no Samantha. We couldn't have done that. See, my brother and I had learned to respect flowers too much to carelessly throw them away. Also, we knew we had been wrong about Mrs. Morney." Grandma walked over to the wagon and then turned to face her granddaughter and her friends.

"Rex and I didn't just learn about caring for flowers and being responsible enough to deal with consequences. We also found out that we had been wrong about the type of person Mrs. Morney was. We made assumptions about her just because she wanted to protect her flowers, which were really important to her."

"Did you become friends with her?" asked Logan.

"I don't know if I would have called us 'friends.' See, my problem had been that I hadn't known enough about her to understand why she was the way she was. I was wrong. I had judged her too quickly," answered Grandma T.

"She still shouldn't have yelled at you and your brother, Grandma," said Sam.

"No, maybe not, but she was lonely too. Sometimes we tend to rush too quickly to conclusions." Grandma grabbed the handle of the wagon and started to pull it back behind the house. She paused and stared at Sam, Logan, and Frankie until she could see they were all looking at her. "It is not our job to make judgments about others. Sometimes we just don't know all the facts." Grandma winked at the three and headed back to her gardening.

Sam and her friends stood up and slowly made their way to the treehouse in silence. Up in the tree they gathered solemnly around the table.

"She doesn't understand," Sam said adamantly. "I know what she was trying to tell us, but she doesn't know all the facts."

"I wonder how she knows what we've been up to," said Logan.

"Oh, come on. She's a grown-up. They always know. My bet, though, is that she doesn't know everything. We probably would have received a little bit more direct talk." Sam dug into her pocket for some gum, but came up empty.

"I think she's right," replied Frankie quietly.

"What! Not you too! Do you remember the green tarp, the rope? How about the knife that Old Man Starn held above you while you were crawling on the ground?!" Sam stood up from the table and went to look out the window towards the lake.

"Sam, I'm not saying that I don't think OMS is up to something." Frankie took off his hat and started to play with the clasp. "I'm just saying that we really don't know OMS. We only know bits and pieces of information. I think we're taking the missing puzzle pieces and hammering them in where we decide they should go."

"I am not talking about puzzles. I am talking about OMS."

"What Grandma T. said about people not understanding others – I know what she means. That's happened to me before where I used to go to school," said Frankie. Both Sam and Logan looked over with interest. Frankie rarely talked about his life before Loon Lake.

"What do you mean?" asked Logan.

"It wasn't much really. I remember we had this big math test and I got all the answers right. I was so excited because I had actually studied for it. My teacher figured I must have cheated so she accused me of it in front of the whole class." Frankie shrugged his shoulders and looked at his friends.

"That's awful," said Sam returning to the table. "What'd you do?"

"I couldn't *do* anything. She was the teacher. I just learned my lesson. I learned that if you throw in a couple of wrong answers every now and then, don't raise your hand too much, they'll leave you alone."

"Wow. You purposefully put wrong answers on your papers?" Logan asked horrified at the idea. "Don't you want to get the best grades you can?"

"Why?" asked Frankie. "Who cares? And besides, what good will it do me if I'm just made fun of?"

Logan just shook his head and sat quietly. Sam was looking at Frankie with a new sense of understanding.

"What about OMS?" asked Logan. "Should we give up and just forget about him?" Logan was secretly hoping that this would be the decision of the group.

"I think we should just continue what we're doing," said Frankie. "We can't just ignore everything we know, but maybe we should just start concentrating on this Saturday and how we are going to beat Derrick in the tournament instead of worrying about OMS."

"I've been giving that some thought," answered Logan. "I have an idea of the strategy we should use."

"I was counting on that," said Sam grinning at Logan. "We can't lose to those creeps."

"If we do, you guys do realize don't you that we will have to go through with putting the fish guts on his steps?" Frankie asked looking from one friend to another.

"Yeah, Derrick and his cousin would kill us," Logan said with a shudder.

"As if they could," Sam said disgustedly. "We aren't going to lose so we won't have to think about it," Sam said confidently.

"Ok, we'll worry about that later," responded Logan. "Right now, let me tell you guys some of the ideas I have for Saturday."

"Good idea," said Sam. "I'm going to go and ask Grandma for some Cokes and snacks to keep us energized." Sam got up and headed off in search of food and drinks.

"Hurry up," hollered Logan after her. "We have a lot of planning to do in the next couple of days." The kids pushed thoughts of OMS out of their heads and instead concentrated on the upcoming fishing tournament.

# Chapter 9

# The Kid Fish Tournament

The Kid Fish Tournament was a big event for Loon Lake locals. A portion of the public boat landing was roped off for registration and weighing in the participants catch. The field across the road from the landing was designated as a parking lot and garage sale of sorts. Many of the Loon Lake families participated in a "community" garage sale every year. They always chose to hold their rummage sale on the day of the Kid Fish Tournament to capitalize on all the parents of the participants that could really do nothing but wait for their child to finish the event. Sam's parents had their own table at the sale filled with partially damaged toys and unwanted clothes.

Sam's dad had entered Sam and Logan into the tournament at The Loon Lagoon (Mr. Meets was sponsoring the tournament, just like he did every year.) Sam's dad was excited about Sam and Logan entering, but he was worried that Frankie would feel left out. He knew how inseparable the three were and didn't want the kids to have hard feelings between them. Sam had assured her dad that Frankie was not upset, in fact, he was going to be in the treehouse watching them with the binoculars.

"There's a lot of people here," said Frankie looking at the crowd near the registration table.

"Yeah. Mr. Meets said that he expected at least 12 different teams to enter into the contest. That's 24 kids participating with at least double that many adults wandering around between the landing and across the road," Logan said, scanning the crowd for his parents.

"Have you guys seen Derrick and his cousin yet?" asked Frankie.

"As a matter of fact, look who just pulled in." Sam stood with her arms across her chest glaring at the brand new truck that had just driven into the landing area. It was pulling an aluminum boat that was loaded with all new equipment. Derrick caught sight of Sam and sneered at her from his passenger window. Sam stuck her tongue out and tossed her head in a different direction.

"Don't worry about him," said Logan. "We have a game plan. We just need to stick to it."

"I am not worried in the least," replied Sam. "The sight of him just makes me sick, that's all."

"When are we supposed to get started?" asked Frankie. He was still new to fishing tournaments and wasn't sure of the procedures.

"They're doing the inspections of the boats and equipment right now," said Logan, pointing over to where a group of three event volunteers were systematically looking through the boats to make sure participants hadn't hidden any fish to try and cheat. Logan glanced at his watch. "We should be starting in about a half an hour."

The rules of the event were fairly simple. Each boat had to be a row boat. (They didn't want kids, even those who had been through a boating safety course, using motors and running into each other.) There could only be two kids in a boat and they needed to have proper life jackets. Also, the kids could take up to three fishing poles in each boat, but they could only have two lines in the water at a time. The only fish that could be kept were bluegills and they would be weighed at the landing. The entire tournament lasted 2 hours. If a boat came in early, their catch would be weighed at that time. A couple of local businesses had donated some money for the first and second place winners.

"Hey kids! Yoo-hoo, over here," Grandma called waving at them from the other side of the fence that separated her property from the landing.

"Sam, your grandma wants us," said Logan starting to walk over to talk to Grandma T.

"Hey Gram, what's up?" asked Sam as her and Frankie walked up to the fence.

"I packed you and Logan a cooler sweetheart," Grandma said passing a small cooler over the top of the fence.

"Great!" said Logan peering into the cooler that was filled with cookies, pop, and pretzels.

"Grandma, we're only going to be gone for a couple of hours," said Sam.

"Nevertheless, you need to eat. I packed a washcloth in the cooler so that you could wash your hands before you grab something to snack on. Also, make sure you go the bathroom too before you go out. You don't want to get out there and then decide you need to come back in just to use the restroom."

"Thanks, Grandma T.," said Logan.

"Yeah, thanks Grandma," said Sam.

"You're welcome. Here Frankie, I packed some cookies and pretzels for you too. Sam's father told me you were going to be up in the treehouse while the tournament was happening." Grandma T. handed Frankie a brown paper bag brimming with goodies. "Before you go up, make sure you grab a Coke off the porch."

"Hey, thanks Grandma T.," replied Frankie enthusiastically opening the bag and grabbing one of the chocolate chip cookies.

"Ok, well I'm off," Grandma Troman said smiling at the kids. "I'm sorry I can't stay and watch, but I have to make a quick trip to the grocery store. I'll be back to see how you do. Good luck." Grandma headed back to her house, giving a quick wave.

"Hey," said Frankie between mouthfuls of cookie. "It looks like they are ready to begin a little early." Frankie was pointing towards the dock area where fathers were helping their sons and daughters put the boats in the water.

"Sam! Logan!" shouted Sam's father. "Let's go, come on." He was heading towards the bank where he had tied up Grandma Troman's row boat earlier that morning.

"It's show time," said Sam, giving Frankie a high five.

"Do we have everything?" Logan anxiously asked. "I don't have the walkie talkie. Do you have it?" Logan was frantically feeling his pockets and looking around the ground as if something fell out.

Sam smiled at Frankie and rolled her eyes. "I've got the radio in my bag," replied Sam holding up the small tote bag she had been carrying. "We've checked and double checked everything. The radios are charged, there's one in the treehouse for Frankie, and we have enough worms from your worm bed to last us three weeks of non-stop fishing if we wanted to. We are set." She gave an encouraging smile to Logan and grabbed his arm to pull him towards the boat. "Let's get going."

"Frankie, you'll be watching Derrick's boat?" asked Logan.

"I'm all set. I'll be giving you regular updates every 10 minutes," assured Frankie as he headed out and around the fence towards the treehouse.

After 15 minutes of chaos, all 12 row boats were in the water. Mr. Meets rang a large cow bell, compliments of Mr. Wheaton, and the tournament started.

Sam and Logan immediately headed straight for Cattail Cove to begin fishing. The three friends had decided that this was the best spot for catching a lot of bluegills at one time. The problem, though, was that many of the fish were smaller than what could be caught in deeper areas of the lake. They also had to spend about 15 minutes rowing over to that side of the lake, and another 15 minutes rowing back to the landing. They were taking a risk, but they were also not expecting to move around a lot unless they absolutely needed to.

"Where is Derrick the Deranged?" asked Sam, rowing as fast as she could.

"It looks like he's anchoring at the drop-off out from the Wheaton's dock," responded Logan. He was trying to shield his eyes from the morning sun to see if he was looking at the right boat. Frankie had the binoculars in the treehouse so that he could spy on Derrick and his cousin.

"There are some big bluegills over there," Sam commented. "That's usually where Dad takes the pontoon boat when he goes out."

"We'll know for sure if it's him when Frankie calls."

A few minutes later, Logan and Sam anchored the boat and started fishing. It wasn't long before they heard Frankie over the two-way radio.

"Treehouse to Red and Rambo. How are you guys doing?"

"We just got our lines in the water. Where's the enemy?" asked Sam.

"He's over by the Wheaton's farm. They've been fishing for about five minutes now and have caught two bluegills."

"Wonderful," remarked Sam sarcastically into the radio. "Are you keeping track?"

"That's affirmative," stated Frankie. He had pulled up the bench to the window facing the lake and was spying on Derrick through the binoculars. Leaning against the wall of the treehouse was a small dry erase board with a line down the middle. One side was for tally marks to count Derrick and his cousin's fish, and the other side was for Logan and Sam.

"We'll call you when we have five in our live net," said Sam putting down the radio so she could reel in a fish.

"Sounds good," came Frankie's voice over the radio.

The first half hour of fishing flew by. Logan and Sam were doing really well. At last count they had 13 fish while Derrick and his cousin had only caught 10. Sam, Logan, and Frankie had all planned on where to go for different fishing spots if it was necessary, but it looked like they were going to be able to stay at Cattail Cove. Another strategy that had been mentioned was the idea of doing a little bit of "sabotage" to Derrick and his cousin. That particular plan really didn't take off since they couldn't agree on it. Logan had been adamantly against it, Frankie had agreed with him saying that they needed to win by their own merit, and Sam had thought the sabotage method had definite possibilities, but she had been over-ruled by the boys.

The second half hour brought less bites, but Sam and Logan were still able to keep ahead of Derrick and his cousin by a handful of fish.

"We've only got about 40 minutes left to catch fish before we need to start heading in," said Logan looking at his watch.

"We're having really good luck," said Sam pulling in another small bluegill.

"You're right, but it could still be close," replied Logan.

Sam put her fish in the live net and then radioed Frankie to tell him to add another fish to their total.

"The two of you are leading the enemy by 5 fish," responded Frankie. "Keep it up."

"How are the other boats doing?" asked Sam.

"I notice people pulling up a fish here and there, but nothing great."

"Okay. We'll get back to you later." Sam put down the radio, wiped her wormy hand on her jeans, and grabbed a cookie out of the cooler.

"What are you doing? We need to be fishing," accused Logan.

"I'm taking a break. You heard Frankie, we're in the lead. Do you want one?" asked Sam lifting up her cookie.

Logan looked over and noticed that Sam had not used the washcloth Grandma Troman had provided. He gave her his best disgusted look. "No thanks, but I'll take a Coke."

Sam grabbed two Cokes out of the cooler and handed one to Logan. She happened to glance towards Old Man Starn's and noticed some movement outside.

"Logan," whispered Sam. "Look over towards the OMS's house." Logan, who was in the process of taking a nice size bluegill off his hook, turned and looked in the direction of Old Man Starn's property.

"I don't see anything," replied Logan tossing the bluegill into the live net.

"Well look closer," whispered Sam forcefully.

Logan looked again and this time noticed OMS walking towards the woods with a chopping ax.

"He's probably chopping wood," stated Logan. "We're not supposed to be worrying about him. We need to be concentrating on fishing. Speaking of which, where is your bobber?"

Sam looked around and noticed that her bobber was completely under water. She hurried to reel in the fish. "We're beating Derrick right now, and that's all that counts," Sam said as she unhooked the fish and threw it in the net.

"In the number of fish, Sam," responded Logan. "All that's going to matter when we get to the weigh-in will be the total weight of the fish. We don't have time to deal with OMS."

"He's in there doing something," said Sam. "We should be watching. For all we know, he could be burying another body. I wish we had binoculars."

"Frankie needed them," said Logan. "Let's just keep fishing."

Sam gave Logan a stony look and returned to her fishing. She alternated her attention between watching the activity in the woods and watching her bobber.

After 15 more minutes of fishing, Sam and Logan were still in the lead with a total of 26 bluegills, while Derrick and his cousin only had 20.

"How much longer before we head in?" asked Sam.

Logan checked his watch. "My alarm should go off in about 20 minutes. That's when we have to start heading back to the landing."

"You set your watch alarm?"

"That's what it's there for," answered Logan.

Sam just shook her head as she reeled in another small bluegill. "I have an idea for something we could do for the next few minutes or so," Sam said hesitantly.

"Everything's going fine right now. Why would you want to change what we're doing?" Logan looked over at Sam and noticed her staring over to OMS's woods. "Oh, no," said Logan. "Let's just keep stay right here. We don't know what's going on over there, but everything is probably fine. Don't you remember Mrs. Morney?"

"We need more facts. We're leading in the number of fish. All I was thinking is that we could take a little detour on our way in to the landing." Sam gave Logan a stubborn look. "Let's buzz Frankie and see if he agrees. That way we could make the decision as a group."

Logan had an uneasy feeling that he was going to be out-voted, but he picked up the radio and two-wayed Frankie.

"Rambo to Shorty, come in Shorty."

"What's up?" asked Frankie over the radio.

"Mystery Man is up to no good."

"What? I don't understand," said Frankie.

"The ax is out of the shed. I repeat, the ax is out of the shed," said Logan.

"Rambo man, I have no clue what you're saying."

Sam grabbed the radio out of Logan's hand rolling her eyes. "OMS is in the woods with an ax."

"Are you serious?! Can you guys see what he's doing? Is he just chopping wood or is something up?" asked Frankie firing questions at his friends.

Logan put his hand out for the radio and Sam reluctantly returned it to him. "We can't see that much from where we're at," said Logan. "We've only got about," Logan looked at his watch and winced, "15 minutes before we need to start rowing in. Sam thought that maybe we should detour over towards his bank to see if we could get a better idea of what he's doing."

"Well, you guys are ahead and it wouldn't hurt to get a better look," responded Frankie.

Sam gave Logan an "I told you so" look and started to reel in another fish.

"Have you caught anymore fish since I last talked to you?" asked Frankie.

"Sam just reeled in another one and I caught one a couple of minutes ago."

"That makes it 28 to 21," said Frankie double checking his dry erase board. "My vote is that we chance it."

"We do have a longer ways to row back," cautioned Logan. "And the tournament goes by weight, not number."

"We would be taking a chance," replied Frankie. "I think it's worth it though with everything else we know about OMS."

Logan sighed, resigned to the fact that they would soon be headed in the direction of Old Man Starn's.

"Okay. We'll head that way, but we aren't going to stay too long. We don't want to be late for the weigh-in."

"Okay. I'll watch for your boat to come around the trees after you're done spying on OMS," said Frankie. He had been switching between talking into the radio and looking towards Derrick's boat. He watched as Derrick pulled in what looked like a very large bluegill. Frankie added the tally to his board, but decided now was not the time to give a report.

Sam and Logan pulled up their anchor and started rowing towards OMS's dock.

"Do you see where he went," asked Sam.

"There's some movement in the woods, but I can't tell what he's doing. Let's float on the other side of his dock and maybe we can get a better view," answered Logan. "I also think we should keep fishing."

"Good idea. We don't want him to suspect anything."

"Actually, I was thinking more about how we need to beat Derrick in the tournament," answered Logan sarcastically.

"Oh. Yeah, you're right."

The friends positioned their boat a little ways from OMS's dock and cast their lines. They decided against using the anchor. The lake was fairly calm and they didn't want to waste the extra time of pulling it in.

"There he is," whispered Sam pointing just to the right of where they had seen him digging a hole a couple of weeks ago.

Logan reeled in a small perch and tossed it back into the water. "I wonder what he's doing," said Logan curiously.

"Maybe he knows we're on to him. Maybe he's going to dig up whoever he killed and bury them somewhere else."

"I doubt it," answered Logan. "Sam, you've got a bite. You're bobber's underwater."

"How can I care about fishing at a time like this?" asked Sam throwing her hands in the air.

"I care. Hand me your pole."

Sam handed over her pole to Logan and continued her watch of the woods. Logan took the pole and reeled in Sam's fish, tossing it into the live net.

"He's coming out of the woods!" whispered Sam.

Logan looked over and, sure enough, Old Man Starn was walking empty handed out towards his garage. He went inside and appeared seconds later with a wheelbarrow.

"He's going to move something," said Sam.

"Wow, you're really good at this detective stuff," replied Logan. Sam just gave him a fake smile and continued to watch the woods.

"What do you think he's doing?" asked Sam.

"I don't know, but it looks like we're going to find out," said Logan pointing towards OMS who was emerging from the woods pushing the wheelbarrow.

"He's heading straight for his shed," said Sam.

"And now he's stacking what appears to be wood on his woodpile," answered Logan.

"Oh, man. I really wanted to catch him this time," said Sam disappointedly.

"I like how his woodpile is nice and neat," said Logan. "Do you see how each piece of wood seems to be the same size so that there aren't a bunch of uneven pieces sticking out?" He looked over at Sam but she was just giving him a weird look so he decided to shut up.

"Oh, no!" said Logan as his watch beeper went off. "We've got to start rowing back."

"Can you shut that thing off?!" said Sam forcefully. She was looking towards OMS who had stopped what he was doing and was looking at their boat.

"The alarm button is stuck," answered Logan who was trying fervently to turn off the annoying sound.

"Put it in the water," said Sam who had jumped into the middle seat and was now rowing as fast as she could in the direction of the landing area.

"You have got to be kidding," answered Logan completely horrified at the idea. "This is my favorite watch."

"Well, fix it then! Everyone is looking at us!"

Logan finally got the sound to stop. He picked up the radio to report in to Frankie. "Rambo to Shorty. We have 2 more to add to our total. How did we do?"

"That gives you guys 30," answered Frankie.

"How many did the enemy catch?" asked Logan.

"Well. They've stopped fishing so that's good. They just pulled into the landing."

"Shorty, how many did they catch?"

"They brought in 28," said Frankie.

"Did they catch a lot of big ones?" asked Logan not feeling too hopeful.

"They didn't do too bad. We'll just have to see what happens. I see you guys coming up towards the other boats. I'm going to head down so I can meet you."

"Okay. We'll see you in a little bit," answered Logan.

"We may still beat him," said Sam shrugging her shoulders.

"I guess," answered Logan in an uncertain voice.

Sam rowed up to the bank of the landing where Frankie was standing and sandwiched her grandmother's boat between some of the others. The kids pulled the boat a little ways up on shore and hurried to get in line at the weigh table.

"Looks like you guys just made it back in time," said Derrick who was ahead of them in line. "A few more minutes and you would have been disqualified."

"We made it here," snarled Sam. "Mind your own business."

Mr. Meets was busy at the table dumping a bucket of fish into his weighing container and then recording the weight onto a large board.

"Not bad, Mackenzie. You and your partner have some nice gills here." Mr. Meets smiled at the Carley twins. "You've got a total of 5.6 lbs. That'll put you in second place right now."

Sam looked at the board. It looked as if the last two boats that needed to weigh in were theirs and Derrick's.

"Well, Mr. Baker," Mr. Meets said as Derrick stepped up to the table. "Let's have a look at what you got." Mr. Meets dumped Derrick's fish into the container. "The two of you had a good day of fishing. We have a new leader in the tournament, folks," Mr. Meets said to some of the participants and their families who were gathered around the table. "Mr. Baker and his cousin here have a total of 8.4 lbs of fish!"

Derrick turned around and smiled at Sam who was looking a little uneasy. "You're turn Carrot Top," said Derrick stepping back to make room for Sam and her friends.

Sam stepped up to the table without replying to Derrick. She lifted her bucket onto the table and waited for the verdict.

"Looks like we're going to have a close one," said Mr. Meets looking at the scales. "It looks like Logan and Sam are our new...2nd place winners with a total of 8.1 lbs of fish!" Mr. Meets slapped Sam and Logan on the back to congratulate them and then turned to do the same to Derrick. Some of the people who were still gathered around clapped and offered their congratulations. Sam and

Logan accepted the $15 dollars in prize money and collected their fish to return to the live net. Derrick and his cousin walked over towards Sam and her friends after receiving their $25 dollars for first place.

"I hope this teaches you children a lesson," said Derrick giving his cousin a high five. "You really should be happy that you even got second place."

"Why don't you go jump in the lake?" suggested Sam.

"A little sensitive, are we? You shouldn't mess with best," sneered Derrick giving Sam and her friends a cocky smile. "And remember," said Derrick pointing his finger at Sam. "I want proof that you losers followed through on your word." He swaggered off with his cousin to receive a congratulatory slap on the back from his father.

"I'd like to go over there and ..." started Sam.

"Hey, Mr. Troman. How are you doing?" Logan asked Sam's dad as he approached them at the weigh-in table.

"Second place, huh? Not too shabby. What are you going to do with your prize money?"

"We don't know yet," mumbled Sam.

"Well, you did a good job. Your mother and I are going to take Katie to the grocery store. Do you want to come or are you going to stay here?" asked Sam's dad glancing at his watch.

"I'll probably stay here. We've got some things to do in the treehouse," replied Sam.

"Okay. Can you return your grandmother's boat to her dock?"

"We'll take care of it, Mr. T.," said Frankie.

"Thanks Frankie. All three of you should come over in a couple of hours. We're going to be having hamburgers and hotdogs on the grill."

"Thanks, Mr. Troman," said Logan. "We'll be there."

Sam's dad headed off in the direction of Sam's house where Katie and Sam's mother were waiting in the driveway.

"What are we going to do?" asked Logan looking at Frankie and Sam.

"We'll figure out something," said Frankie. "It looks like we'll be making another trip to Old Man Starn's after all."

# Chapter 10

# A Pail of Problems

Choosing the appropriate day and time to go to OMS's was a difficult decision. Frankie had wanted to carry out the operation at night, but both Logan's and Sam's parents would not have allowed them to be away after dark. The same was true for early in the morning. They would have to go during the day, and this created a problematic situation.

After striking out with ideas, the kids went over to Sam's house to eat hotdogs and returned to the treehouse later to continue brainstorming.

"This isn't working," said Sam feeling defeated. They had just thrown out a plan that involved firecrackers and Halloween costumes. All of the friends were feeling frustrated and tired after such a long morning.

"You guys, let's go down to The Loon Lagoon and buy some potato chips with part of our reward money." Sam stood up from the treehouse bench and stretched her arms in the limited ceiling space. "I want to get out of here for awhile."

"We're not getting anywhere," answered Logan. "I wouldn't mind going for a walk."

"Fine with me," said Frankie. He went over and removed the rug from the floor in the treasure room. Frankie grabbed a few one dollar bills from the vault and then replaced the floor boards and the rug.

The walk to the store was a somber one. The three friends were each wondering how they were going to carry out the consequences of the dare without getting caught or killed. They were not in the best of spirits when they entered The Loon Lagoon.

"Hello, guys," said Mr. Meets. "Did you decide to come in and spend some of that prize money you won this morning?"

"Hi, Mr. Meets," said Sam. "We came in to get a bag of chips."

"Well, this is the right spot for that. Did you and Logan enjoy fishing in the tournament?"

"It was a lot of fun," answered Logan.

"It's too bad, Frankie, that you couldn't be in the boat as well. Maybe some year we'll have to change the rules to allow three people in the boat."

"That's okay," replied Frankie. "I still had a good time watching everyone out on the lake."

"That's good. I'm glad to hear it," said Mr. Meets as he stacked boxes behind the counter.

"What's this, Mr. Meets?" asked Logan pointing to a flyer that was hanging lopsided on the bulletin board near the door.

"What's what?" asked Mr. Meets looking up from his work. "Oh, that. That flyer's about the meeting being held in the township hall this Monday afternoon. It ought to be a real humdinger of a meeting, let me tell you." Mr. Meets brought a box from around the counter and began to stock some of the food items The Loon Lagoon carried.

"What's the meeting about," asked Sam going over and standing next to Logan to get a look at the flyer.

"Probably nothing you three would be interested in. There's a chemical plant that wants to build a factory in the area. It would help give some people jobs, but there are people that say it would hurt the quality of water in Loon Lake." Mr. Meets finished what he was doing and came over to stand with the kids.

"Hey, I think I heard my dad talking about that," replied Sam.

"I wouldn't be surprised," responded Mr. Meets. "I know that a lot of lake people and many others will be going to that meeting. A lot of them have been stopping in here to tell me they will be there to hear what is said."

Frankie gave a deliberate look to Sam and Logan. "Who's going to be there, Mr. Meets?"

"Oh, pretty much everyone. I know the Wheatons are going, Martha Mayflower, the Bakers, Tom Starn, Sam's parents and grandmother, the Taylors, practically the whole neighborhood.

"Hopefully the plant won't build around here," said Logan putting their bag of chips on the counter.

"I'm with you on that, Logan," said Mr. Meets. "I don't want anything to hurt our lake."

"How long do these meetings usually last?" asked Sam. "The flyer says it starts at 4:00 P.M., but doesn't give an ending time."

"That's hard to say. A typical town meeting lasts an hour or so, but I'm guessing that this one will last longer. Are you guys thinking of coming? It would be a good experience for all of you."

"I think we're going to be busy," said Frankie. "Maybe we'll come to the next one."

"Okay, but you don't know what you're missing," replied Mr. Meets, handing Logan back his change.

"Thanks, Mr. Meets. We'll see you later," said Sam as she headed out the door.

"Bye kids," said Mr. Meets waving as they disappeared outside.

"What do you guys think?" Sam asked her friends as they headed out of the parking lot.

"I think we were just given the best time and day to carry out our fish guts mission," answered Frankie.

"I think you're right," replied Logan. "We'd still be taking a risk, though. He may decide not to go or he could come back early."

"Yeah, but it's the best idea we have so far," said Sam opening the bag of chips.

"We have some planning to do," said Logan.

Sam grinned and looked at Frankie. "I didn't doubt it for a minute," Sam said offering the open bag of chips to Logan. "Let's head back and get started."

The three spent what was left of the afternoon planning and debating on how to best get the pail of fish guts onto Old Man Starn's front steps. They parted that evening with plans to meet at the treehouse Monday around 3:00 P.M.

The time flew quickly for Logan and Frankie. Neither of them was looking forward to what lay ahead. Sam, however, was a little too eager to carry out the mission. She was the first one at the treehouse Monday afternoon.

"Hey, Sam, what are you doing?" asked Logan as he and Frankie climbed up the ladder. Logan and Frankie had both left bikes at the base of the tree near Sam's.

"Waiting for you," stated Sam popping a bubble with her gum.

"Did you get the fish guts," asked Frankie plopping down in the bean bag chair.

"Yeah. Dad always buries the fish guts in our backyard under some pine trees. I found an old tin bucket in the back of the garage under a pile of junk and put a couple shovels of guts in that."

"Nice," said Frankie. "I bet they smell pretty good."

"The bucket is out in the boat with a board over it. I figured that was the one place Grandma wouldn't accidentally see it."

"Good idea," said Logan. "We're planning on leaving the pail at OMS's though. Are you sure your mom won't discover that it's missing?"

"Nah. She hasn't been in that part of the garage in ages and Dad has his own buckets that he uses. This was an old pail Mom used to use when she had a vegetable garden. We haven't had one of those in forever."

"Did you check to see if we had film in the camera?" asked Logan sitting down at the table with a pile of notes.

"We have two pictures left," answered Sam. "We're all set."

"How do you think Derrick's going to take it when he sees the picture of the pail of fish guts on OMS's steps?" asked Frankie. "Don't you think he's expecting us to *dump* out the fish guts so that we make a mess?"

"That wasn't our bet," said Sam. "Derrick's wager was that the loser had to put a pail of fish guts on Old Man Starn's steps without getting caught. That's what we're going to do."

"Well, how about this? What if we put the pail on the steps, take the picture, and then bring the pail back with us? We'll show Derrick the picture and he'll never know

that we removed the pail after the picture was taken."
Frankie looked at Sam and Logan to see what they thought.

"I didn't even think about that," said Logan. "That would be a great way to follow through with the wager and not stir up too much trouble."

"I want to stir up trouble," Sam said. "He needs to know we're on to him."

"It'd be safer to bring the pail back," replied Logan hoping to talk Sam into the idea.

"Look. We're not making a mess. We're just giving him a warning. We need to leave the pail there to make a statement." Sam crossed her arms and glared at Logan.

Frankie shrugged his shoulders, "That's fine with me. It was just an idea."

"Okay. We'll leave the pail there," said Logan knowing that there was no budging Sam when she was determined about something.
Logan looked at his watch. "We've got about 20 minutes before we need to start riding our bikes towards OMS's."

The friends had decided that they had a better chance of being successful riding bikes than they did walking. They could make a faster getaway if needed and all three did ride their bikes every now and then so it wouldn't look too suspicious. Frankie had told Sam and Logan about a spot across the road from OMS's driveway that could easily hide their bikes and themselves. He told his friends he had hid there a few times when he wasn't ready to go home. Frankie thought it would be easy to wait there for Old Man Starn to leave for the meeting. OMS didn't have any close neighbors so the kids only had to worry about people in their cars seeing them go into the hiding spot.

"What are you doing?" Frankie asked Logan who was rapidly writing at the table.

"I'm writing a 'just in case' letter," said Logan who paused for a moment and then resumed.

"I'm afraid to ask, but what is a 'just in case' letter?" asked Sam coming over to read behind his shoulder.

"Hey!" exclaimed Sam before Logan had a chance to answer. She snatched the paper from Logan. "This is in case something happens to us."

"Well. You can never be too sure," answered Logan grabbing the paper back. "When Frankie went last time, the two of us were here to get help if we needed it. This time no one will know where we are. If they can't find us, they'll check the treehouse. I'll leave this letter that explains everything in the middle of the table."

"What if one of our parents comes looking for us soon after we leave?" asked Sam.

"I hadn't thought about that," admitted Logan. "I really don't think that's going to happen. You're parents and mine both know we're going to be riding our bikes. Besides that, they will be at the meeting along with your grandma. I guess I didn't think about Frankie's mom, though."

"I wouldn't worry," answered Frankie. "My mom knows I'm with friends, but I doubt she even knows where you live, let alone where the treehouse is."

"We'll have to risk leaving it," said Logan. "We can't go over to someone's house that may have killed another person without leaving behind a note." He finished the letter and placed it squarely in the center of the table. "I also made a hand-written flyer about 'Fluffy.' I figured we could show that to anyone if we were caught, and just say we were following up on our search." Logan showed his friends the quick flyer he had made with a quick description of 'Fluffy' and Frankie's old phone number. "It won't explain the pail of fish guts, but it will give us an excuse for being on OMS's property."

"I like that. You can be pretty sneaky when you want to," Sam grinned at Logan and grabbed the camera from the table. "Let's get going."

"We're still early," Logan commented looking at his watch again. "I guess we could go and get to our hiding spot."

"I'm ready," said Frankie finishing a Coke that he had brought with him.

The three friends headed down the ladder and onto their bikes. Sam rode up to the house and met Grandma heading out.

"I'm off to town, Samantha," said Grandma zipping her purse shut. "I want to pick up a movie at the store before I head over to the township hall."

"We're going on a bike ride, Grandma," said Sam.

"Your father told me you had your bike with you. Be careful, honey."

"We will. Have fun at your meeting." Sam waved goodbye to her Grandmother as she backed her car out of the driveway. Frankie and Logan rode up beside her.

"Did you get the fish guts?" asked Sam.

"I have them with me," replied Frankie holding up the tin pail.

"I've got the camera in my bike basket. Grandma didn't even notice it."

"I have the fake flyer in my pocket, and I have my whistle," said Logan holding up a whistle that was hanging on a string around his neck.

"A whistle?" asked Sam.

"Yeah. You know. It's to make noise in case he comes after us or something," said Logan hiding stuffing it under his shirt.

"You are *really* good at this," said Sam. "You should think about becoming a detective or something."

"I don't think so," said Logan adamantly. "Too many problems."

Sam and Frankie laughed and the three headed down the road in fairly good spirits.

It didn't take long before the friends found the spot Frankie had mentioned. After quickly making sure no one was looking, Sam and Logan hid their bikes in some weeds and followed Frankie under the branches of a large, overgrown pine tree.

"Cool! How did you ever find this place?" asked Sam looking around.

"It's pretty awesome, isn't it?" replied Frankie.

"We're totally hidden under here. I can't believe there's this much room under this old tree." Sam walked around the base of the tree. It was like being under a gigantic hoop skirt made of pine needles.

"We have a great view of OMS's driveway. Hopefully he hasn't left yet. I want to see him leave so that we'll know for sure he's gone." Logan brushed some pine needles away from a space on the ground and sat down to keep watch out for OMS. Frankie and Sam joined him on the ground.

"Maybe we should have left earlier," commented Logan looking again at his watch. "It's 3:38. He may have left already."

"The hall isn't that far from here," said Frankie. "Let's just sit and wait for awhile."

The three sat and waited patiently for the next 10 minutes without seeing any activity from Old Man Starn's driveway.

"Maybe we should just go and get this over with," said Sam.

"Hold on.  Get down.  I hear something," whispered Logan.

Frankie had heard the noise too, because he was already crouched down peering between the prickly branches.

"It's him.  Look," whispered Frankie pointing to the battered red truck that was slowly coming down the drive.

The three continued to scrunch to the ground until they saw OMS turn out of his driveway and disappear out of sight.

"Come on," said Sam standing up and brushing herself off.  "Let's head out."

"Wait," said Frankie.  "Let me go and get my bike. I'll go out to the road and check if it's clear.  I'll give you a thumbs-up if no one's coming."  Frankie gave a quick look in both directions, and then, grabbing the pail full of fish guts, he left the hiding spot to pick up his bike and wait in the ditch.  Seeing that no one was coming, Frankie gave the thumbs-up sign and his friends quickly scrambled out to join him.

"Quick, let's go," said Sam and the three quickly rode down Old Man Starn's driveway.  They slowed down after they reached the first bend that hid them from the road.

"How much farther is it?" whispered Logan.

"Not far.  Are you doing okay?" asked Frankie glancing back at Logan who appeared to be a little pale.

"Yeah, I'll be fine," responded Logan in a very nervous voice.

"No offense, but I think you're a 'behind the scenes' type of guy," Frankie said to Logan.

"I agree completely," muttered Logan, wishing he was home in his room reading a book.

"Hey guys. This is it." Sam had stopped her bike near the trees that lined the driveway. Up ahead was the house looking pleasingly empty.

"Sam, grab the camera and come with me," said Frankie grabbing the pail of fish guts. "Logan can stay here and be a lookout."

Sam hurried to follow Frankie to the steps. "Whoops," she said looking down at the camera.

"Whoops!" said Logan in a loud whisper. "What do you mean 'Whoops?'"

"I bumped the button on the camera by mistake. Relax. I have one picture left. Now you have a souvenir." Sam took the developing picture from the front of the Polaroid camera and turned to hand it to Logan. "Um, Logan. I really think you should sit down. You don't look too good."

"Please," begged Logan. "Just go and take the picture."

"Yeah. Okay. I'm going. We'll be out of here in no time." Sam ran to where Frankie was positioning the pail of guts on the steps.

"Step back, Frankie, or you'll be in the picture," said Sam.

"It doesn't matter to me. Just take the picture with enough of the house to make sure Derrick knows we were here."

Sam snapped the picture and grabbed it away from the camera. "Operation complete. Let's hit the road." Sam ran back to where she had left Logan, who was still sitting on his bike looking a little dazed. Frankie caught up to them and the three headed back down the driveway.

"We're not safe yet," whispered Logan frantically looking in all directions. "We need to get out of this driveway without anyone seeing us."

The friends slowed down when they came to the last bend that would put them in sight of the road.

"Do you see anyone," whispered Sam.

"I don't think anyone's coming. I don't hear anybody," replied Frankie.

The three friends stood quietly listening intently for any sound of cars. Just then, a loud crash came from the direction of the woods.

"What was that? Is he coming for us?" whispered Logan anxiously looking from one direction to the next.

"Logan, it was a raccoon. Look." Frankie was pointing where a raccoon was moving through a section of trees.

"Let's get out of here," said Sam giving a meaningful look to Frankie and nodding towards Logan.

"I'm with you. We're going to chance it." Frankie took one more quick look and then darted out towards the road. Sam and Logan were right behind him. The three did not stop to talk until they had ridden all the way back to the treehouse.

"I have never been so excited to see your grandma's place," said Logan as they rode into the driveway.

"Me neither," said Sam propping her bike against the back porch and following her friends to the willow tree.

Logan, Sam, and Frankie climbed the ladder and gathered around the table in the treehouse, looking at the two pictures Sam had taken. Logan had already picked up the 'just in case' letter and had thrown it into the trashcan after ripping it into little pieces.

"That's a nice picture of the bike basket," said Frankie smiling at Sam.

"I was practicing," replied Sam as Logan let out a groan.

"What do you think he's going to do when he finds the pail of fish guts?" asked Logan.

"I don't know. We left them in the pail so we didn't damage anything. He'll probably just wonder who did it and then bury them." Sam shrugged her shoulders and grabbed a piece of gum out of her pocket.

"Tomorrow we can walk over to Derrick's house and see if he's home," said Logan. "We'll be done with him after we show him the picture."

"Good idea," said Frankie.

"What are we going to do with the rest of the afternoon?" Sam asked her friends.

"Let's go down to the dock, hang our feet in the water, and catch some fish," suggested Frankie.

"I'm in. I'll do anything as long as it doesn't involve going to OMS's again," replied Logan. The three friends laughed and headed down to the dock.

# Chapter 11

# Dog Gone Wrong

It was Wednesday. Two days had gone by since the friends had paid a "visit" to Old Man Starn. They were on their way to The Loon Lagoon to buy candy to take with them out on the boat. Yesterday, they had shown the picture of the fish guts on OMS's steps to an extremely smug Derrick. Having that distasteful deed out of the way, the three friends then destroyed the evidence by burning the picture in a trashcan up in the treehouse. The kids were glad that they were done with the fish guts mission, but they were still very concerned about the activities of OMS.

"I'm telling you," said Logan kicking a stone down the road, "if OMS is up to something, he'll mess up sooner or later. The bad guys always slip-up and are brought to justice in my mystery books."

"But he could strike again," argued Sam, frustrated with the situation. She couldn't believe that with all of their hard work, they had still been unable to come up with solid evidence to prove his guilt.

"I wonder how he has been able to evade the police for so long. Do you think this was his first killing?" inquired Frankie.

"I just can't believe we could have a bona fide murderer living here at Loon Lake," said Logan.

Sam, Logan, and Frankie all walked into the store with troubled minds. They went around to the candy aisle and began to debate on what to buy for their fishing trip that afternoon. Frankie thought they should get some licorice, Logan wanted M&Ms, and Sam wanted some gum to replenish her shrinking supply in the treehouse. The friends had just decided to buy all three when they heard the door bells jingle, announcing a new customer.

"Get down," whispered Frankie pulling on Sam and Logan's arms. He held a finger to his lips and pointed towards the door of the store.

"Hello Tom," greeted Mr. Meets as Old Man Starn walked in and approached the counter. "What can I help you with today?"

"I need to pay for my gas," replied OMS counting out some money from his wallet.

"That'll be $20," said Mr. Meets taking the money from Old Man Starn. "Hey, I just heard about your hit-and-run a couple of weeks ago."

Hearing this piece of news, three heads popped around the candy display.

OMS grunted. "I took care of it."

"Bob Wheaton was in the store just the other day telling me about it." Mr. Meets rang up the gas purchase and handed the receipt to OMS. "He sure was sorry to lose Rascal. He's had him for over 12 years. It's sad, but I guess that's how it goes."

"Rascal?" Frankie whispered to his friends. "The German Shepherd?"

"He was pretty torn up about it," Mr. Meets continued. "Bob said he's been burying dead animals for years, part of being a farmer, but he just couldn't do it with ol' Rascal."

"It was nothing. Just a hole," replied Old Man Starn. He turned his head slightly to the right in the direction of the candy aisle. Three heads quickly retreated back into hiding. Old Man Starn stuffed his receipt into his pocket and started heading towards the door.

"By the way," said Mr. Meets. "I sure liked those cucumbers you brought by. You grow some of the best vegetables around. What's your secret?"

OMS shrugged and gave a mysterious smile. "Plenty of fish guts mulched into the soil. It helps bring out the flavor." He glanced over in the direction of the three eavesdroppers and winked. Seeing this, the three friends quickly moved farther back into the aisle, bumping candy bars off the shelf in their haste.

"Really," said Mr. Meets skeptically. He was oblivious to the interaction between OMS and the kids. "That's interesting. I'll have to keep that in mind. See you later."

"Goodbye," said Old Man Starn as he walked out of the store, headed for his truck.

"Come on," said Logan haphazardly grabbing some candy off the shelf. "We gotta get out of here so we can talk."

Sam, Logan, and Frankie approached the counter with their selections. Sam looked out the window and saw OMS climb into his truck and head off down the road.

"So, you three picked out what you want?" questioned Mr. Meets ringing up their order.

"Yeah. We're set," replied Frankie.

"Mr. Meets? Can I ask you a question?" asked Sam. "Were you talking with Mr. Starn about Mr. Wheaton's old dog?"

"I'm sorry to say that I was. Didn't you guys hear about it?" Mr. Meets shook his head sadly and handed Logan back the change. "Someone hit the poor animal and left him out by that bend near Tom's house. The county really needs to look at changing the speed limit over there. There are so many trees in that area that it's hard to spot animals as they get near the road."

"Wow. I can't believe Rascal is dead," said Logan. "He was always kinda part of the neighborhood."

"Well, he was older than you guys and for dog years, that's pretty good." Mr. Meets finished putting their candy in a small brown bag and handed the bag to Frankie. "Rascal had a good lake life. A dog can't ask for anything better."

"Yeah. I guess so," replied Sam waving to the store owner as she walked out the door.

Frankie and Logan said their goodbyes to Mr. Meets and followed Sam into the afternoon sunshine. The three were quiet as they walked across the parking lot. Frankie was the first to recover from hearing the news.

"Boy, were we wrong," said Frankie grabbing a stick from the ditch and trailing it behind him as he walked. "Old Man Starn didn't kill anyone, and he *knows* about the fish guts. We're in trouble."

"I don't think we did very well as detectives," agreed Logan. He was feeling guilty at the moment about the pail of fish guts they had left on OMS's doorstep. "What are you thinking about, Sam?" He looked over at Sam who was being unusually quiet.

"I just can't believe it. It was a dog all along." Sam kicked a rock as the kids turned into Grandma Troman's driveway and headed for the treehouse. "I never thought about it being a dog. We knew he didn't own one."

Sam, Logan, and Frankie climbed up the ladder and gathered around the table. Frankie emptied the contents of the brown bag onto the table, but none of the friends seemed interested in the candy. The scheduled fishing trip was long forgotten.

"What do you think he's going to do about the fish guts?" asked Frankie.

"I don't think he'll do anything. He probably just suspects it's us because of all the time we've spent fishing over by his house." Sam propped her elbows on the table and rested her chin in her hands. "He can't blame us without knowing for sure."

"Grandma T. was right," said Frankie leaning back against the wall. "We thought we knew him, but we didn't."

Logan picked up the brown bag and meticulously started to fold it, smoothing out any wrinkled edges. "We're being too hard on ourselves. We saw something weird happening and we checked into it. We did some stakeouts, we went to his house without getting caught, and now we know he's not a murderer."

"We better hope he doesn't tell Grandma T. about the fish guts," said Logan smiling at his friends. "We may just find ourselves spending a couple of Saturdays helping OMS with his flowers." The three friends grinned at one another and tore into the candy.

# Chapter 12

# Independence Day

That following Saturday was Independence Day. Sam, Logan, and Frankie had spent most of their morning, and a little bit of the afternoon, in Oakdale with Sam's parents. The three friends had a great time in town watching the parade, walking through town, and even riding on some small carnival rides that were brought into Oakdale for the Independence Day celebration. They had also gathered enough candy at the parade to stock the treehouse for quite awhile.

Independence Day was Grandma Troman's favorite holiday. She always held an annual Fourth of July party. She invited family members and lake neighbors to gather at her house for food, fun, and fireworks. The party began in the early evening and lasted well after the grand finale of the fireworks show that was launched over the lake every year. Grandma T. loved a good party so when she gave one, she went all out.

By the time evening had set in, Grandma's yard resembled a very festive gathering place. Tiki torches and colorful lanterns had been positioned around the yard in anticipation of the late night. Sam's dad had started a bonfire in the campfire ring out by the lake. The picnic table was dragged over towards the fire along with some plastic yard chairs that had been stacked in a corner of the garage. Folding tables had been moved into the screened-in porch and were heavy with food. Family members and neighbors were milling around eating, laughing, and occasionally arguing with one another good-naturedly.

The three friends had wanted to barricade the treehouse against intruders, but Sam's dad said that wouldn't be polite. Faced with no other option, Sam, Logan, and Frankie had placed any valuables (which included their candy stash and binoculars) into the vault for safe keeping. They had also decided that they would take turns being on "treehouse duty" so they could give supervised tours instead of allowing nosy and annoying cousins free reign. Logan lost the first round of rock, paper, scissors so he had to take the first shift.

"Do you want us to bring you a hotdog?" Sam asked Logan. She and Frankie were getting ready to head to the porch to grab something to eat.

"I'd rather have a hamburger if there are any left," replied Logan. "And maybe some of that pudding stuff your Aunt Bobbie makes."

"Okay. We'll be back," answered Sam as the two began to snake their way through the groups of people to the food area.

"Hi kids," said Grandma Troman when the pair finally made it to the porch. Grandma T. was busy pouring party nuts into a chipped polka dotted bowl.

"Hi, Grandma. We thought we'd grab something to eat. We're going to take Logan some food too." Sam grabbed two paper plates and began working on filling them up. Frankie's plate was already half full.

"Is Logan guarding the treehouse?" asked Grandma, smiling at the pair.

"Uh-huh," answered Frankie with his mouth full. "He's under strict orders not to let in any destruction-seeking cousins."

"Yes, well…I don't blame you kids for being cautious." Grandma looked over her shoulder where Martha Mayflower had cornered Mrs. Wheaton, and was talking her ear off. "Every now and then a person has to open their home to others if they want to be neighborly, but that doesn't mean they have to like it."

"Grandma, how come you invited Mrs. Mayflower?" Sam asked glancing over to where Mr. Wheaton had just rescued his wife, and was now leading her towards the punch table.

"Sam, believe me, I thought long and hard about that one." Grandma grabbed three cookies and put one on each of the plates Sam and Frankie were carrying. "It's better that she's here instead of stewing on the other side of the fence wondering what we're up to. You have to pick your battles, Sam, and not inviting her to my party was not one I wanted to start."

"Well, at least she didn't bring her horde of cats with her," said Frankie.

"You're right, dear. We can be thankful for that." Grandma T. grabbed the empty nut container and a platter with nothing left on it except for cookie crumbs. She headed towards the door, but stopped when she remembered something. "Oh, Frankie, I forgot. Martha is looking for you. I don't know what she wants though. I didn't ask. I'm sure she'll corner you sometime tonight." Grandma turned and headed off in the direction of the kitchen.

"I wonder what she wants," said Sam leading the way back to the treehouse.

"Well, I can wait until later to find out. Right now I'm starved."

"You're always starved," replied Sam.

"Samantha! Honey, over here," Sam's mom was waving her over to the picnic table area where she was sitting with Sam's little sister, Katie.

Sam reluctantly changed directions and headed over to see what her mom wanted. Frankie followed, eating a hotdog on the way.

"Samantha, I need to go and make some more punch. Katie wants to go and see the treehouse, and I need you watch her for a little while." Sam's mom grabbed a napkin and wiped Kool-Aid off of her younger daughter's face.

"But mommm! We just grabbed our food. Do I have to take her now?" pleaded Sam.

"Samantha, I really need you to do this for me. Just for a little while. Your Grandmother's punch bowl is bone dry and she can't handle everything all by herself. Take Katie for a little while and I'll be sure to collect her in an hour or so."

"Fine. I'll take her." Sam glared at her little sister who was playing with the ruffles of her ridiculously puffy pink dress.

"Thanks, honey. I'll see you guys later. Don't forget to make sure she doesn't go anywhere near the water." Sam's mom headed off towards the direction of the punch bowl table leaving Katie in her sister's care.

"Come on, Katie Baby. Let's go." Sam handed Frankie Logan's plate and grabbed her sister's sticky hand with her free one.

"I no hold hands," said Katie stomping her feet. "I big girl."

"Fine. We're going to the treehouse. Come on." Sam nudged her sister to get her to start walking while she followed close behind.

After the trio made it to the willow tree, it took a few minutes to get the food and Katie up the ladder. Once this was accomplished, the three friends sat at the table to eat (Frankie was almost done) while Katie investigated the treehouse.

"Why'd you bring your sister, Sam?" Logan asked, beginning to chomp down on a dill pickle.

"Mom made me." Sam glanced over to where her sister was sitting on the bean bag chair and stuck her tongue out at her.

"Oh, Sam. Leave her alone. She's behaving right now." Frankie looked over and smiled at Katie. He always wondered what it would have been like to have brothers or sisters.

"Katie, would you like to play with the flashlight?" Frankie got up and went over to grab the flashlight off the shelf. He turned it on and handed it to Katie.

"I want light! I want light!" Katie took the flashlight and made her way around the treehouse for a second time, only this time she was pointing the dim light every which way.

"We'll give her a few more minutes and then I'll go take her to Dad," said Sam, watching her little sister crawl around on the floor in her new dress.

"Are you going to eat that cookie?" asked Frankie coming back to the table and pointing at the chocolate chip cookie on Sam's plate.

"No, go ahead and take it." Sam pushed her plate in Frankie's direction and looked over at Logan. "Why are you being so quiet, Logan?"

"I don't know. I was just thinking about how glad I am that all that stuff with OMS is over with." Logan got up and grabbed the three empty plates, smashing them down into the already over-flowing trash can. "I keep thinking that we should have brought back the pail with the fish guts."

"Oh, it doesn't matter. We know that he knows it was us and he hasn't sent the police after us or anything." Sam shrugged her shoulders. She wouldn't admit it to her friends, but she was a little worried, though not enough to let it ruin her Fourth of July fun.

"Sammy," whined Katie, coming over to tug on Sam's shirt. "Me want to go down."

"I think that's a great idea," said Sam grabbing the flashlight out of Katie's hand and putting it on the table. "Let's go and find Dad."

"I'll take treehouse duty," said Frankie plopping down on the beanbag after grabbing a magazine off of Logan's bookshelf.

"Ok. I'll be back after I return the little monster," said Sam, tugging playfully on Katie's hair.

"I think I'm going to go and find my mom and dad," stated Logan. "I'm supposed to be checking in every now and then."

"If you go by the potato chips, can you grab me some?" Frankie looked up from the magazine and smiled sweetly at his friends.

Logan said he'd take care of it and then went down the ladder first so that Sam could hand down Katie. Once they were on the ground, Logan headed in the direction of the house while Sam and Katie walked over to the fire pit where Sam had spotted her dad.

"Hello, girls. What have you been up to?" asked Sam's dad, looking up from his camp chair.

"I go in tree," answered Katie proudly, skipping the rest of the way to her father.

"Did you have fun, Pretty Girl?" Sam's dad asked Katie, picking her up and putting her on his lap.

Katie nodded and snuggled under his arm while popping her thumb into her mouth.

"Dad. I took her up in the tree since Mom told me I had to. Can I leave her with you now?"

"Go ahead," said Sam's dad, sympathizing with his older daughter. "I'll keep her here with me for awhile. Maybe we'll roast marshmallows or something."

"Thanks Dad!" said Sam, turning quickly and running back towards the treehouse before he could change his mind. She wanted to spend some time up in the tree, spying on party guests from the window.

The evening went by quickly. The kids spent most of the time in the treehouse, but they did come down to play a couple of games of beanbags. Sam's dad had built the boards for the game the summer before and Grandma T. had sewn the bean bags. The game was played a lot like horseshoes. Sam and her friends enjoyed the yard game because they were allowed to be on teams with the aunts, uncles, and other grown-ups. It wasn't just an adult thing like euchre, a card game that Sam's family played every now and then.

After Sam and Logan lost a game of beanbags to Frankie and Mr. Meets, the three friends headed back up to their post in the treehouse. They had decided to spy on Mrs. Mayflower as she made her way around the yard, talking to anyone who would listen to her.

"Look," said Frankie motioning to Mrs. Mayflower down by the dock. "She's now talking to your Aunt Bobbie."

"Let me see." Sam stuck her head in the window and grinned. "Aunt Bobbie can't stand her. I know 'cause her and my mom were talking last Christmas about who they were going to send Christmas cards to. Aunt Bobbie said that she wasn't going to send one to 'that nosy busybody' no matter how inhospitable it was."

"She's now talked to over half the people here," replied Logan, writing Aunt Bobbie's name to a list he was making of people Mrs. Mayflower had somehow or another pulled into a conversation. He had neatly printed at the top of the paper; *Casualties of the Mayflower: The Untold Story.*

"I think I'm going to go and get some punch," stated Sam, putting down the binoculars that the kids had retrieved from the vault.

"Logan and I might come down in a little bit too. We don't really need to keep too much of a watch on the treehouse now." Frankie fell into the beanbag chair and grabbed his hat that had been lying on the floor and put it on.

"We really should go down sometime soon Frankie, and see what Mrs. Mayflower wanted to talk to you about." Logan glanced over at Frankie and then looked out the window again. He spotted Mrs. Mayflower talking to Shirley, the mail lady, and added the name to the growing list of 'victims.'

"I was afraid you weren't going to forget about that," groaned Frankie. "You may as well add our names to your piece of paper."

Logan smiled as he did just that.

"I'm out of here," Sam said, heading down the ladder. She took a winding route to the punch table, skirting around neighbors and family, keeping a big distance between herself and Mrs. Mayflower.

"Hi Grandma," Sam said as she approached the table. Her grandma was fidgeting with the napkins and cups, making sure that everything looked nice. Sam grabbed a cup and started to dip the punch into her cup, deliberately skimming a good portion of the raspberry and orange sherbet off the top. The ice cream her grandma added to the punch was what Sam considered the best part, especially when it melted and made a rainbow swirl in the punch bowl.

"Are you having fun, dear?" Grandma asked, dipping a cup of punch for herself. "Did you get a chance to play some beanbags?"

"Yeah. Logan and I lost to Mr. Meets and Frankie." Sam took a drink of her punch, leaving a frothy ice cream mustache on her upper lip.

"I was wondering if you could do me a favor," Grandma said, smiling at her granddaughter and handing her a napkin.

"Anything," replied Sam. She quickly finished her cup of punch and used the napkin to wipe her mouth clean.

"I would like you to take some punch over to Mr. Starn. He's been over there sitting by the lake for awhile now, and I haven't had a chance to go say hi to him yet."

Sam whipped her head around and for the first time saw what was indisputably OMS sitting in a chair by the water.

"Oh, Grandma! I can't go over there. He doesn't like me!" Sam looked pleadingly at her grandma, while panicking inside at the thought of approaching Old Man Starn.

"That's complete nonsense! Samantha Patricia Troman, you can go over there and you will. I am asking you for a favor. You can't possibly say he doesn't like you when he doesn't even know you."

"Grandma, I really don't think this is a good idea." Sam began to crinkle her plastic cup nervously.

"Sweetheart. You can do this. You need to do this." Grandma T. smiled and gave Sam a quick, reassuring hug. "Go on now. Don't forget the punch," said Grandma T., dipping out a cup and handing it to Sam.

"Okay, Gram," answered Sam meekly, beginning to slowly make her way across the yard trying to prolong the inevitable.

"Um, hi Mr. Starn," Sam said, handing a cup of punch to him trying to make sure her fingers didn't accidentally touch his. "Grandma thought you may want something to drink."

"Thanks," he said, grabbing the cup and taking a drink. Old Man Starn glanced at the rowboat tied to the dock. "Have you kids been catching any fish lately?"

"Yeah. Some."

"Well, I guess maybe you guys had other things on your mind." OMS gave Sam a questioning look.

"I know it was Rascal in the tarp," Sam blurted out before she could stop herself.

OMS raised his eyebrows and nodded, taking another sip of his punch. He didn't say anything.

Sam looked at the ground and started making a hole in the dirt with the toe of her old tennis shoe. She was wishing she had never gone over to the punch bowl in the first place. Sam could feel her insides twist up like an old telephone cord. She wanted to confess about the fish guts since they both *knew* about it, but she didn't know how to start. She decided to take the advice her grandma always gave her and just get the unpleasantness done with.

"Mr. Starn," said Sam, looking up from the ground and taking a deep breath. "Frankie, and Logan, and I...well...we left the fish guts on your porch. See, it was a dare and we had to do it, because we couldn't possibly back down from that creep, Derrick. He's the guy that dared us, you see. We lost the Kid Fish Tournament to him and putting the fish guts on your steps was what the loser had to do. I know I shouldn't have agreed to the dare. I wasn't thinking and Grandma always says that's going to be my downfall. And also," continued Sam, hurrying on before she lost her nerve, "at the time we thought you were an evil murderer and we wanted to protect the neighborhood so we had to kinda keep an eye on you. You understand, don't you?" Sam looked at OMS and nervously waited to hear what he had to say.

"I guess you can't blame a person for trying to protect others." Old Man Starn swirled the rest of his punch and then finished it. "I am glad that the fish guts we left *in* the bucket." OMS winked at Sam and tossed his empty cup in a nearby trashcan. "I guess you need to brush up on your fishing skills."

"I wasn't paying too much attention to my fishing that day," Sam said defensively. "I'm actually pretty good at fishing when I try really hard." Sam was a little upset about OMS thinking that she needed to practice her fishing techniques.

"Your grandma has told me that you are pretty good at casting a line. She was bragging about you the other day at the market. I guess she must really be proud of you."

"I didn't know she talked to you about me." Sam was awed by the idea.

"A person never knows everything. It's the stuff that's not said that is sometimes the most important." OMS looked out at the calm lake. "You know, Sam. I think the two of us are kind of alike."

"What do ya mean?" Sam asked, not sure what traits they could possibly share.

"We both love Loon Lake. We both like to fish, and we both go our own way sometimes." Old Man Starn smiled at Sam. "We may have to get together and go fishing sometime." OMS laughed at the terrified look on Sam's face. "Don't worry, we can wait until we know each other a little better and I promise I'll leave all of my sharp knives at home. Thanks for the punch. I think I'm going to get going now."

"You're not staying for the fireworks?" Sam asked, surprised that she was actually beginning to enjoy her conversation with him.

"I'll watch them from my dock. I thought I might go out and go bullhead fishing."

"Good luck." Sam smiled at OMS and turned to head back to the treehouse as Old Man Starn ambled to his truck. She caught sight of her Grandma, standing next to the porch smiling at her. Sam waved at Grandma T. and continued on to the willow tree. Frankie and Logan were walking straight towards her.

"What's that?" asked Sam when her friends approached. Frankie had what appeared to be a tiger striped cat in his arms. It ironically looked very similar to the stray cat that Sam had thought of when writing the description of "Fluffy" on the flyer. When Frankie and Logan got closer she could see that it was indeed the cat with only half an ear on one side.

"Don't you recognize Fluffy? Mrs. Mayflower found him and was very happy to return him to me," answered Frankie with a grin. "She found him in her live trap that she had set to try and catch a raccoon that had been eating all of the birdseed in one of her birdfeeders." Frankie was clutching the cat and looked as if he couldn't be happier. Logan was just shaking his head in amazement.

"Oh, and guess what? Fluffy is a He," Frankie said, smiling down at the ball of fur in his arms. "Mrs. Mayflower thought it was odd that I didn't know if my own cat was a male or female. I thought she was going to start giving me the third degree, but I was able to keep the conversation short."

"How'd you manage that?" asked Sam.

"He asked her how she knew Fluffy was a boy," Logan said with a smile. "She shut right up. I guess she didn't want to explain."

Sam laughed. It was always nice to rile up Mrs. Mayflower.

"Good one. Well, what are we going to do now? You're not going to keep him are you?" asked Sam.

"Nope. Not me, us. I figured we could be parents to the poor guy. It only seems right to give him a home," stated Frankie. He was scratching "Fluffy's" ear and the cat seemed to be enjoying every minute of it.

"I guess we could have Dad put some type of cat door in the treehouse. We might even be able to rig up a walkway so that Fluffy can get up and down easily." Sam was already thinking about how they could convert the treehouse into a type of "home" for the cat.

"I bet your grandma would feed him, Sam," stated Logan. "She's talked before about having a cat. Her house and the treehouse could be his home for right now, at least until we figure out what to do with him in the winter."

With the issue of Fluffy somewhat hashed out, Sam began to tell her friends about the conversation she had with Old Man Starn. Frankie and Logan were both surprised that OMS took Sam's confession so well.

"I hate to say it again, but Grandma T. was right," said Frankie.

"I know. And the bad thing is I kinda like him." Sam was as shocked by her feelings as her two best friends.

"Is that what I think it is?" asked Logan pointing to something positioned directly under the ladder of the treehouse. All three friends stopped and stared at the sight of the pail they had left on OMS's steps.

Sam quickly turned around and scanned the driveway to see if Old Man Starn was still there. She saw him standing next to his red truck, looking in their direction. Sam waved and smiled. OMS waved back and then climbed into his truck to leave.

"Hey!" yelled Frankie. "There's a note."

Logan and Sam hurried to the willow tree and peered over Frankie's shoulder.

Keep Fishing - OMS

"How does he know we call him Old Man Starn?" asked Sam looking at Frankie who was laughing as if the note was the funniest thing he had ever read.

"I think we should just give it up, Sam," replied Logan. "Somehow grown-ups just seem to find out these things."

"Hey, look! The fireworks are starting!" Frankie pointed up to the sky where the fading, purple lights were leaving an outline in the sky resembling an elegant ball gown.

"Let's head over towards the dock." Logan placed the bucket back on the ground under the tree and led the way over to the water.

The three friends stretched out on the grass, gazing at the array of colors bursting in the sky above them. The night was almost perfect, with a slight breeze and very few mosquitoes.

"Almost half the summer is gone," said Frankie, turning his head to look at Logan and Sam.

"But you're forgetting, over half of the summer is left," replied Sam. She didn't even want to begin thinking about school starting back up until she absolutely had to.

"So much has happened already with OMS, Rascal, and now Fluffy," said Logan, glancing at the cat that was perched on Frankie's stomach. "I wonder what's going to happen next."

"Whatever happens, we'll be ready. This is our lake and our summer vacation. We're going to fish, swim, and enjoy ourselves." Sam propped herself up on an elbow and looked out at the lake. The Grand Finale of the fireworks show was just finishing. The reflection on the lake was absolutely beautiful. Many of the family members and neighbors were still scattered in the yard, heads turned towards the sky. Sam couldn't help but think about how lucky she was to be sitting on the grass with her friends, looking out at Loon Lake. She felt like the night was magical. Life couldn't get any better than it was right now.

Made in the USA
Monee, IL
05 December 2022

19783447R00069